OTTO PENZLER PRES
AMERICAN MYSTERY CL

THE FABULOUS CLIPJOINT

FREDRIC BROWN (1906-1972) was a prolific writer of multiple genres, including mystery, sci-fi, poetry, and non-fiction, whose work has been championed by Stephen King, Philip K. Dick, Umberto Eco, and many more literary luminaries. In the mystery world, he is best remembered today for his series of mysteries featuring Ed and Am Hunter, who made their first appearance in the Edgar Award winner, *The Fabulous Clipjoint.*

LAWRENCE BLOCK is a Mystery Writers of America Grand Master who has been writing award-winning mystery and suspense fiction for over half a century. In addition to creating several popular and long-running series characters (such as Matthew Scudder, Bernie Rhodenbarr, and Keller), Block's novels include dozens of standalone mysteries, as well as other titles in a range of genres.

THE FABULOUS CLIPJOINT

FREDRIC BROWN

Introduction by
LAWRENCE BLOCK

**AMERICAN
MYSTERY
CLASSICS**

Penzler Publishers
New York

Published in 2021 by Penzler Publishers
58 Warren Street, New York, NY 10007
penzlerpublishers.com

Distributed by W. W. Norton

Cover image: Andy Ross
Cover design: Mauricio Diaz

Paperback ISBN 978-1-61316-254-5
Hardcover ISBN 978-1-61316-253-8

Library of Congress Control Number: 2021944422

Printed in the United States of America

9 8 7 6 5 4 3 2 1

THE FABULOUS
CLIPJOINT

INTRODUCTION

I WAS only nine years old in 1947, when *The Fabulous Clipjoint* was published, so it was probably another eight years before I read it. I discovered Fredric Brown during my freshman year at Antioch College, and I must have read a half-dozen of his Bantam paperbacks, along with a few hundred other books I tore through back then. Most of the others had at least some claim to consideration as serious literature, which was a phrase that meant rather more to me than it does now, but I don't know that anything I read was more engaging or entertaining than Fredric Brown's fiction, and even then I knew that was important.

Was *The Fabulous Clipjoint* one of those early reads? It seems likely, but I can't be sure. I remember a few other Brown novels I read very early on—*The Screaming Mimi, The Wench is Dead, Here Comes a Candle*—but whether I read *Clipjoint* then or a little later is impossible to say.

Because two years later, an even ten years after its publication, I had dropped out of Antioch to work as an assistant editor at a literary agency in New York. I had actually sold a few short crime stories of my own and decided that my progress in this field could only be enhanced by increasing my familiarity with what others had written.

Since I was writing and selling short crime fiction, I set out to read my way through all the back copies I could find of *Manhunt* and its imitators. A Times Square shop on Eighth Avenue had a huge stock of back-date magazines, priced at two for 25¢, and I wasn't making much money, but a five-dollar bill went a long way there. I also wanted to read crime novels, so I bought a batch of paperbacks around town, but then I discovered The Mercantile Library on East 47th Street, just a block from my office.

I've no idea what it cost to be a member, but it couldn't have been much, and the place was heaven for an aficionado of popular fiction. They bought all the new hardcover mysteries, but here's what was remarkable—*they never got rid of anything!* The Collier brothers were more likely to part company with a dead cat than was the Merc to deaccession a ten-year-old mystery novel.

Well, I was in pig paradise. I worked all day reading the earnest efforts of fee-paying wannabes, the vast majority of whom could not write their names in the dirt with a stick, and then I went home with a stack of hardcover novels by people at the other end of the scribbler spectrum.

I would find a writer—I may well have found him first in one of those back-number magazines—and then I would read one of his novels, and if I liked it I'd read everything he wrote. I remember that David Alexander was one writer who got this treatment. A reporter for the old *Morning Telegraph*, a newspaper for horse players, Alexander wrote a string of novels about one Bart Hardin, a Broadway habitué who lived above a flea circus and wore colorful vests. I guess he also solved crimes. I've largely forgotten the books, though rather less utterly than the world has, but I remember learning that the author had a quirk at least as eye-popping as his hero's waistcoats; he wrote each of his books in the first person, to give it a sense of immediacy and then deliberately rewrote it in the third person, to give it—

Well, I disremember that part, but he must have had his reasons. You know, I'm not sure I believe Alexander actually did this, and even if he did it once I doubt that he did it again. But who knows?

I read, as you may imagine, a lot of books, and made the acquaintance of a considerable body of authors. But when I think back, what I mostly remember is reading my way through the complete works of Fredric Brown. (Or as complete as they were at the time. The man himself was still very much an active writer in 1958, regularly turning out novels and short fiction.)

When, thanks to the Mercantile Library, I was able to return to my residential hotel with Fredric Brown for company, I knew I was in good hands and that a satisfying evening was assured. Some of the man's books were better than others, to be sure, but he himself was unfailingly good company. And what more, really, can one ask of an author?

One thinks inevitably of that annoying passage from Salinger, wherein Holden Caulfield muses on the pleasure to be found in calling up an author after having enjoyed his book. I didn't have fantasies of phoning Fred Brown, or anyone else, but it did strike me from time to time that he was a man whose company I would very likely enjoy.

One time, at the end of a long week, I came home with a bottle of Jim Beam as well as a new-to-me Fredric Brown novel. Halfway through the first chapter, the lead character had a drink. That struck me as a good idea, so I followed his lead— and, as I read on, I took a drink every time the protagonist did.

Don't try this at home.

Oh, I had a feeling Fred Brown and I would get along just fine. And it seemed possible that, in the fullness of time, our paths might well cross. I was beginning to know several science fiction writers who, if they didn't know Brown, had friends in common with him.

This didn't happen. What happened, instead, was Life Itself; I went back to school, left school permanently, married, had children, and went on with the business of becoming myself, whoever that might turn out to be. I still read each new Fredric Brown novel as it came out, but in 1963, the year my second daughter was born, Brown published his final novel, *Mrs. Murphy's Underpants*, and *The Shaggy Dog and Other Murders*, his final short story collection.

He lived another nine years, and died in 1972 at the age of 65. I can't seem to find anything about his final years, even in the age of Google and Wikipedia, and I'm not inclined to probe too deeply.

Before I forget, I should point out that the Mercantile Library is still a very special institution all these years later. There came a time when it expanded its programming and redefined itself as The Center for Fiction, and a few years later relocated into much larger and quite elegant quarters in Brooklyn. It was always a haven, and it's significantly better than ever and, if you can conveniently do so, you should make its acquaintance.

Oh, right.

The Fabulous Clipjoint.

It was Brown's first published novel, and won him an Edgar Allan Poe award for best first novel. (In Mystery Writers of America's early years, that was the only award given for book-length works of fiction. My guess is that those early members realized competition among them for Best Novel would likely

lead to bloodshed. Of course, all these years later, the organiza-
tion has matured, and mean-spirited infighting within its ranks
is quite inconceivable. We have all of us come a long way.)

Clipjoint was also the first installment of a seven-book series, and one wonders if Brown knew when he began it that he'd
want to write more about Ed Hunter and his Uncle Ambrose.
My guess—and who's to say me wrong?—is that he found while
writing the book that he liked the narrative voice and the way
the two men played off each other, so why not find new adven-
tures for them?

Or perhaps whoever took the book on at Dutton urged its
author to undertake a series. That kind of suggestion can be
persuasive, especially when it's made by someone with a check-
book. (A similar suggestion by editor Bucklin Moon led Don-
ald E. Westlake to keep his antihero Parker alive at the end of
The Hunter, and we have him to thank for two dozen unparal-
leled books.) In any event, *The Dead Ringer* followed a year later,
and they kept coming, all the way to *Mrs. Murphy's Underpants.*

Clipjoint's plot has echoes of *Hamlet,* and there's probably an
implausibility to be encountered within its pages, but nothing
that ever bothered me.

In the fall semester of 2019, I served as writer-in-residence at
Newberry College; in addition to a writing workshop, I taught
"Reading Mystery Fiction for Pleasure." I can't call it a great
success; what I failed to realize is that reading for pleasure is no
longer an option when one is a student. Reading all too quickly
becomes a burden, and academic survival depends upon getting
through books as quickly as possible and retaining just enough
to appear to have read it.

Still, I exposed my students to some good books, and *The
Fabulous Clipjoint* was one of them. I guess they liked it well

enough, although it's hard to know what they made of a book written seventy-plus years before it found its way to them.

Never mind. I got to read it again, and enjoyed it again, if in a slightly different way than the first time around. If you're renewing an acquaintance with the book, I think you'll find it holds up well. If you're coming upon it for the first time, I expect you'll enjoy it.

And, if this is in fact your introduction to Fredric Brown, I have to say I envy you. You're about to make the acquaintance of a man who never fails to be excellent company.

Just don't try to match him drink for drink...

—LAWRENCE BLOCK
Greenwich Village

CHAPTER 1

IN MY DREAM I was reaching right through the glass of the window of a hockshop. It was the hockshop on North Clark Street, the west side of the street, half a block north of Grand Avenue. I was reaching out a hand through the glass to touch a silver trombone. The other things in the window were blurred and hazy.

The singing made me turn around instead of touching the silver trombone. It was Gardie's voice.

She was singing and skipping rope along the sidewalk. Like she used to before she started high school last year and got boy-crazy, with lipstick and powder all over her face. She was not quite fifteen; three and a half years younger than I. She had make-up on now, in this dream of mine, thick as ever, but she was skipping rope, too, and singing like a kid, "One, two, three, O'Leary; four, five, six, O'Leary; seven, eight . . ."

But through the dream I was waking up. It's confusing when you're like that, half one way and half the other. The sound of the elevated roaring by is almost part of the dream, and there's somebody walking in the hallway outside the flat, and—when the elevated has gone by—there's the ticking of the alarm clock on the floor by the bed and the extra little click it gives when the alarm is ready to explode.

I shut it off and rolled back, but I kept my eyes open so I wouldn't go back to sleep. The dream faded. I thought, I wish I had a trombone; that's why I dreamed that. Why did Gardie have to come along and wake me up?

I thought, I'll have to get up right away. Pop was out drinking last night and still wasn't home when I went to sleep. He'll be hard to wake up this morning.

I thought, I wish I didn't have to go to work. I wish I could take the train to Janesville to see my Uncle Ambrose, with the carnival. I hadn't seen him for ten years, since I was a kid of eight. But I thought about him because Pop had mentioned him yesterday. He'd told Mom that his brother Ambrose was with the J. C. Hobart carney that was playing Janesville this week and that was the nearest they'd get to Chicago, and he wished he could take a day off and go to Janesville.

And Mom (who isn't really my mom, but my stepmother) had got that looking-for-trouble look on her face and asked, "What do you want to see that no-good bastard for?" and Pop had let it go. Mom didn't like my Uncle Ambrose; that was why we hadn't seen him for ten years.

I could afford to go, I thought, but it would make trouble if I did. I figured like Pop did; it isn't worth it.

I got to get up, I thought. I swung out of bed and went into the bathroom and spattered water into my face to get wide awake. I always used the bathroom and dressed first, and then I woke Pop and got us some breakfast while he got ready. We went to work together. Pop was a linotype operator and he'd got me on as an apprentice printer at the same shop, the Elwood Press.

It was a gosh-awful hot day, for seven in the morning. The window curtain hung as stiff as a board. It was almost hard to breathe. Going to be another scorcher, I thought, as I finished dressing.

I tiptoed along the hall toward the room where Pop and Mom slept. The door to Gardie's room was open and I looked in without meaning to. She was sleeping on her back with her arms thrown out and her face without any make-up on it looked like a kid's face. A kind of dumb kid.

Her face, looking like that, didn't match the rest of her. I mean, maybe because it had been such a hot night she'd taken off her pajama tops and she had nice, round, firm breasts. Maybe they'd be a little too big when she got older but now they were beautiful and she knew it and was proud of them. You could tell that by the way she wore tight sweaters so they would show.

She really is growing up fast, I thought; and I hope she's smart because otherwise she'll be coming home knocked up one of these days, even if she isn't fifteen yet.

She'd probably left her door wide open on purpose so I'd look in and see her that way, too. She wasn't my sister, really, see; not even a half sister. She was Mom's daughter. I'd been eight and Gardie a snot-nosed brat of four when Pop had remarried. My real mom was dead.

No, Gardie wouldn't miss a chance to tease me. She'd like nothing better than to tempt me into making a pass at her—so she could raise hell about it.

I went on past her open door thinking, damn her, damn her. There wasn't anything else I could think or do about it.

I stopped in the kitchen long enough to light a fire under the kettle so it would start to boil for coffee, and then I went back and rapped softly on the door of their bedroom and waited to see if I'd hear Pop move.

He didn't, and that meant I'd have to go in and wake him. I hated to go into their bedroom, somehow. But I knocked again and nothing happened, so I had to open the door.

Pop wasn't there.

Mom was on the bed alone, asleep, and she was dressed all but her shoes. She had on her best dress, the black velvety one. It was awful mussed now and she must have been pretty tight to go to sleep with it on. It was her best dress. Her hair was a mess, too, and she hadn't taken her make-up off and it was smeared and there was lipstick on the pillow. The room smelled of liquor. There was a bottle of it on the dresser, almost empty and with no cork in it.

I looked around to be sure Pop wasn't anywhere at all in the room; and he wasn't. Mom's shoes lay in the opposite corner from the bed, quite a ways apart as though she'd thrown them there from the bed.

But Pop wasn't there.

Pop had never come home at all.

I closed the door even more quietly than I'd opened it. I stood there a minute wondering what to do, and then—like they tell you a drowning man will grab at a straw—I started to look for him. Maybe he came home drunk, I told myself, and went to sleep somewhere in a chair or on the floor.

I looked all over the flat. Under the beds, in the closets, everywhere. I knew it was silly, but I looked. I had to be sure he wasn't anywhere there; and he wasn't.

The water for coffee was boiling away now, spouting out

steam. I turned off the fire under it, and then I had to stop and think. I guess I'd stalled by hunting, so I wouldn't have to think.

I thought, he could have been with somebody, one of the other printers, maybe. He might have spent the night at somebody's place because he got too drunk to get home. I knew I was kidding myself; Pop knew how to hold liquor. He never got that drunk.

But I told myself, maybe that's what happened. Maybe Bunny Wilson? Last night was Bunny's night off; he worked the night shift. Pop often drank with Bunny. A couple of times Bunny had stayed at our place; I'd found him asleep on the sofa in the morning.

Should I phone Bunny Wilson's rooming house? I started for the phone, and then stopped. Once I started phoning, I'd have to go on. I'd have to phone the hospitals and the police and carry through with all of it.

And if I used the phone here, Mom or Gardie might wake up and—well, I don't know why that would have mattered, but it would have.

Or maybe I just wanted to get out of there. I tiptoed out and down one flight, and then I ran down the other two flights.

I got across the street and stopped. I was afraid to phone. And it was almost eight, so I'd have to do something quick or be late to work. Then I realized that didn't matter; I wasn't going to work today anyway. I didn't know what I was going to do. I leaned against a telephone pole and felt sort of hollow and light-headed as though I weren't quite all there, not all of me.

I wanted it over with. I wanted to *know* and get it over with, but I didn't want to go to the police and ask. Or was it the hospitals you called first?

Only I was afraid to call anybody. I wanted to know and I didn't want to know.

Across the street, a car was slowing down. There were two men in it, and the one on the outside was leaning out looking at street numbers. It stopped right in front of our place, and the two men got out, one on each side. They were coppers; it was written all over them, even if they didn't wear uniforms.

This is it, I thought.

Now I'm going to know.

I went across and followed them into the building. I didn't try to catch up; I didn't want to talk to them. I just wanted to listen when they started talking.

I followed them up the stairs, half a flight behind. On the third floor one of them waited while the other walked down the hall and looked at numbers on doors. "Must be next floor," he said.

The one at the head of the stairs turned and looked at me. I had to keep on coming. He said, "Hey, kid, what floor's fifteen on?"

"Next one," I said. "Fourth floor."

They kept on going, and now I was only a few steps behind them. Like that we went from the third floor to the fourth. The one just ahead of me had a fat behind and his trousers were shiny in the seat. They stretched tight every time he took a step up. It's funny; that's all I remember about how they looked, either of them, except that they were big men and coppers. I never saw their faces. I looked at them, but I never saw them.

They stopped in front of fifteen and knocked, and I kept on going right past them and up the flight to the fifth, the top, floor. I kept on going until I reached the top and took a few steps, and then I reached down and pulled off my shoes and went back halfway down the stairs, keeping out of sight back against the wall. I could hear and they couldn't see me.

I could hear everything; I could hear the shuffle of slippers as Mom came to the door; I could hear the door creak just a little as it opened; and in the second of silence that followed, I could hear the ticking of the clock in the kitchen through the opened door. I could hear soft, barefoot steps that would be Gardie coming out of her room to the turn in the hall by the bathroom where, without being seen, she could hear who was at the door.

"Wallace Hunter," said one of the coppers. His voice was rumbly like an el car a long way off. "Wallace Hunter live here?"

I could hear Mom start breathing faster; I guess that was enough of an answer, and I guess the look on her face must have answered his "You—uh—Mrs. Wallace Hunter?" because he went right on. "'Fraid it's bad news, ma'am. He was—uh—"

"An accident? He's hurt—or—"

"He's dead, ma'am. He was dead when we found him. That is—we think it's your husband. We want you to come and identi—that is, as soon as you're able. There's no hurry, ma'am. We can come in and wait till you're over the shock of—"

"How?" Mom's voice wasn't hysterical. It was flat, dead. "How?"

"Well—uh—"

The other copper's voice spoke. The voice that had asked me what floor fifteen was on.

"Robbery, ma'am," he said. "Slugged and rolled in an alley. About two o'clock last night, but his wallet was gone so it wasn't till this morning we found out who—*Catch her, Hank!*"

Hank must not have been fast enough. There was a hell of a loud thud. I heard Gardie's voice, excited, then, and the coppers going on in. I don't know why, but I started for the door, my shoes still in my hand.

It closed in my face.

I went back to the stairs and sat down again. I put my shoes on, and then I just sat there. After awhile someone started down the stairs from the floor above. It was Mr. Fink, the upholsterer, who lived in the flat directly over ours. I moved close against the wall to give him plenty of room to pass me.

At the bottom of the flight, he stopped, one hand on the banister post and looked back at me. I didn't look at him; I watched his hand. It was a flabby hand, with dirty nails.

He said, "Something wrong, Ed?"

"No," I told him.

He took his hand off the post and then put it on again. "Why you sitting there, huh? Lost your job or something?"

"No," I said. "Nothing's wrong."

"Hell there ain't. You wouldn't be sitting there. Your old man get drunk and kick you out or—"

"Let me alone," I said. "Beat it. Let me alone."

"Okay, if you want to get snotty about it. I was just trying to be nice to you. You could be a good kid, Ed. You oughta break away from that drunken bum of a father of yours—"

I got up and started down the steps toward him. I think I was going to kill him; I don't know. He took a look at my face and his face changed. I never saw a guy get so scared so quick. He turned around and walked off fast. I stayed standing there until I heard him going down the next flight.

Then I sat down again and put my head in my hands.

After awhile I heard the door of our flat open. I didn't move or look around through the banister, but I could tell by voices and footsteps that all four of them were leaving.

After all the sound had died away downstairs, I let myself in with my key. I turned on the fire under the kettle again. This time I put coffee in the dripolator and got everything ready. Then I went over to the window and stood looking out across the cement courtyard.

I thought about Pop, and I wished I'd known him better. Oh, we'd got along all right, we'd got along swell, but it came to me now that it was too late, how little I really knew him.

But it was as though I was standing a long way off looking at him, the little I really knew of him, and it seemed now that I'd been wrong about a lot of things.

His drinking, mostly. I could see now that that didn't matter. I didn't know why he drank, but there must have been a reason. Maybe I was beginning to see the reason, looking out the window there. And he was a quiet drinker and a quiet man. I'd seen him angry only a few times, and every one of those times he'd been sober.

I thought, you sit at a linotype all day and set type for A & P handbills and a magazine on asphalt road surfacing and tabular matter for a church council report on finances, and then you come home to a wife who's a bitch and who's been drinking most of the afternoon and wants to quarrel, and a stepdaughter who's an apprentice bitch.

And a son who thinks he's a little bit better than you are because he's a smart-aleck young punk who got honor grades in school and thinks he knows more than you do, and that he's better.

And you're too decent to walk out on a mess like that, and so what do you do? You go down for a few beers and you don't intend to get drunk, but you do. Or maybe you did intend to, and so what?

I remembered that there was a picture of Pop in their bedroom, and I went in and stood looking at it. It was taken about ten years ago, about the time they were married.

I stood looking at it. I didn't know him. He was a stranger to me. And now he was dead and I'd never really know him at all.

When it was half-past ten and Mom and Gardie hadn't come back yet, I left. The flat had been an oven by then, and the streets, with the sun coming almost straight down, were baking hot too. It was a scorcher all right.

I walked west on Grand Avenue, under the el.

I passed a drugstore and I thought, I ought to go in and phone the Elwood Press and tell them I wasn't going to be in today. And that Pop wouldn't be there either. And then I thought the hell with it; I should have phoned at eight o'clock and they know by now we're not coming.

And I didn't know yet what to tell them about when I'd be back. But mostly I just didn't want to talk to anybody yet. It wasn't completely real, like it would begin to be when I'd have to start telling people, "Pop's dead."

It was the same with the police and thinking and talking about the funeral there'd have to be, and everything. I'd waited for Mom and Gardie to come back, but I was glad they hadn't. I didn't want to see them, either.

I'd left a note for Mom telling her I was going to Janesville to tell Uncle Ambrose. Now that Pop was dead, she couldn't say anything about my telling his only brother.

It wasn't so much that I wanted Uncle Ambrose; going to Janesville was mostly an excuse for getting away, I guess.

On Orleans Street I cut down to Kinzie and across the bridge, and down Canal to the C&NW Madison Street Station. The next St. Paul train that went through Janesville was at eleven-twenty. I bought a ticket and sat down in the station and waited.

I bought early afternoon editions of a couple of papers and looked through them. There wasn't any mention of Pop, not even a few lines on an inside page.

Things like that must happen a dozen times a day in Chicago, I thought. They don't rate ink unless it's a big-shot gangster or somebody important. A drunk rolled in an alley, and the guy who slugged him was muggled up and hit too hard or didn't care how hard he hit.

It didn't rate ink. No gang angle. No love nest.

The morgue gets them by the hundred. Not all murders, of course. Bums who go to sleep on a bench in Bughouse Square and don't wake up. Guys who take ten-cent beds or two-bit partitioned rooms in flophouses and in the morning somebody shakes them to wake them up, and the guy's stiff, and the clerk quickly goes through his pockets to see if he's got two bits or four bits or a dollar left, and then he phones for the city to come and get him out. That's Chicago.

And there's the jig found carved with a shiv in an areaway on South Halsted Street and the girl who took laudanum in a cheap hotel room. And the printer who had too much to drink and had probably been followed out of the tavern because there'd been green in his wallet and yesterday was payday.

If they put things like that in the paper, people would get a bad impression of Chicago, but that wasn't the reason they didn't put them in. They left them out because there were too many of them. Unless it was somebody important or somebody died in a spectacular way or there was a sex angle.

Like the percentage girl who probably took the laudanum

somewhere last night—or maybe it was iodine or an overdose of morphine or, if she was desperate enough, even rat poison—she could have had a day of glory in the press. She could have jumped out of a high window into a busy street, waiting on a ledge until she got an audience gathered, and the cops trying to get her back in, and until the newspapers had time to get cameramen there. Then she could have jumped and landed in a bloody mess but with her skirts up around her waist as she lay dead on the sidewalk for a good pic for the photographers.

I left the newspapers on the bench and walked out the front door and stood there watching the people walk by on Madison Street.

It isn't the fault of the newspapers, I thought. The papers just give these people what they want. It's the whole goddam town, I thought; I hate it.

I watched the people go by, and I hated them. When they looked smug or cheerful, like some of them did, I hated them worse. They don't give a damn, I thought, what happens to anybody else, and that's why this is a town in which a man can't walk home with a few drinks under his belt without getting killed for a few lousy bucks.

Maybe it isn't the town, even, I thought. Maybe most people are like that, everywhere. Maybe this town is worse just because it's bigger.

I was watching a jeweler's clock across the street and when it got to be seven minutes after eleven, I went back through the station. The St. Paul train was loading, and I got on and got a seat.

It was as hot as hell in the train. The car filled quickly and a fat woman sat beside me and crowded me against the window. People were standing in the aisles. It wasn't going to be a good trip. Funny, no matter how far down you are mentally, physical discomforts can make you feel worse.

I wondered, what am I doing this for anyway? I should get off, go home, and face the music. I'm just running away. I can send Uncle Ambrose a telegram.

I started to get up, but the train began to move.

CHAPTER 2

THE CARNIVAL LOT was mechanized noise. The merry-go-round's calliope fought with the loudspeakers on the freak show platform, with the thunder of an amplified bass drum booming out a call to bally for the jig show. Under the bingo top a voice called numbers into a microphone and could be heard all over the lot.

I stood in the middle of it all, still stalling, wondering if I could find Uncle Ambrose without having to ask for him. I remembered only vaguely what he looked like. And all I knew about what he did with the carney was that he was a concessionaire. Pop had never talked about him much.

I'd better ask, I decided. I looked around for somebody who wasn't busy or wasn't yelling, and saw that the man at the floss-candy pitch was leaning against an upright, staring at nothing. I walked over and asked where I could find Ambrose Hunter.

He jerked a thumb down the midway. "Ball game. Milk bottle one."

I looked that way. I could see a fat little man with a moustache reaching over the counter, holding out three baseballs at some people who were walking by. It wasn't Uncle Ambrose.

But I walked over anyway. Maybe my uncle hired him, and he could tell me where my uncle was. I got closer.

My God, I thought, it *is* Uncle Ambrose. His face was familiar now. But he'd been so much taller and—well, to a kid of eight, all grownups seem tall, I suppose. And he'd put on weight, although I could see now that he wasn't really fat, like I'd thought at a first look. His eyes, though, were the same; that was how I knew him. I remembered his eyes. They sort of twinkled at you, like he knew something about you that was a secret, and was funny as hell.

Now I was taller than he was.

He was holding the baseballs out to me now, saying, "Three throws for a dime, son. Knock 'em down and win a—"

Of course he couldn't know me; you change so much from eight to eighteen nobody could possibly know you. Just the same, I guess I was a little disappointed that he didn't know me.

I said, "You—you wouldn't recognize me, Uncle Ambrose. I'm Ed. Ed Hunter. I just came from Chicago to tell you—Pop was killed last night."

His face had lighted up like he was really glad to see me when I'd started, but it sure changed when I finished. It went slack for a second, and then it tightened up again, but in a different shape, if you know what I mean. There wasn't any twinkle in his eyes, and he looked like a different guy entirely. He looked, just then, even less like I'd remembered him to be.

"Killed how, Ed? You mean—"

I nodded. "They found him in an alley, dead. Rolled. Payday night and he went out for some drinks and—" I thought there wasn't any use going on. It was obvious from there.

He nodded slowly, and put down the three baseballs in one of the square frames on top of the low counter. He said, "Come on, step over. I'll let down the front."

He did, and then said, "Come on, my quarters are back here." He led the way back past the two boxes on which the dummy milk bottles which you were supposed to knock off with the baseballs were stacked, and lifted the sidewall at the back.

I followed him to a tent pitched about a dozen yards back of his concession. He opened up the flap and I went in first. It was a tent about six by ten feet at the base, with walls that came up straight for three feet and then tapered to the ridge. In the middle you could stand up comfortably. There was a cot and a big trunk at one end, and a couple of canvas folding chairs.

But the first thing I'd noticed was the girl asleep on the cot. She was small and slender and very blonde. She looked about twenty or twenty-five, and even asleep her face was pretty. She was dressed except that she'd kicked off her shoes and she didn't seem to be wearing much if anything under the cotton print dress.

My uncle put his hand on her shoulder and shook her awake. He said, when her eyes opened, "You got to beat it, Toots. This is Ed, my nephew. We got to talk here, and I got to pack. You go get Hoagy and tell him I got to see him right away and it's important, huh?"

She was pulling on her shoes already, wide awake. She'd waked up quickly and completely in a second, and she didn't even look sleepy. She stood up and smoothed down her dress, looking at me.

She said, "Hi, Ed. Your name Hunter, too?" I nodded.

"Get going," my uncle said. "Get Hoagy for me."

She made a face at him, and went out.

"Gal with the posing show," my uncle said. "They don't work till evening, so she came in here for a nap. Last week I found a kangaroo in my bed. Yeah, no kidding. John L., the boxing kangaroo—in the pit show. With a carney, you can find *anything* in your bed."

I was sitting in one of the canvas chairs. He'd opened the trunk and was putting stuff from it into a battered suitcase he'd pulled out from under the cot.

"Y'in there, Am?" a deep voice yelled from outside.

"Come on in, Hoagy," my uncle said.

The flap lifted again, and a big man came in. He seemed to fill the front end of the tent as he stood there, his head almost touching the ridgepole. He had a flat, completely expressionless face.

He said, "Yeah?"

"Look, Hoagy," my uncle said. He stopped packing and sat down beside the suitcase. "I got to go to Chicago. Don't know when I'll get back. You want to take over the ball game while I'm gone?"

"Hell, yes. I'm sloughed here and ten to one I'll be sloughed in Springfield. And if Jake gets a chance to use the blow after that, let him get a cooch. What cut you want?"

"No cut," said my uncle. "You'll have to give Maury the same slice I give him, but the rest is yours. All I want is, you keep my stuff together till I get back. Keep track of my trunk. If I don't get back before the season ends, store it."

"Sure, swell. How'll I keep in touch with you?"

"General Delivery, Chicago. But you don't need to. Nobody's sure of the route past Springfield, but I can follow you in *Billboard*, and when I get back I get back. Okay?"

"Hell, yes. Have a drink on it." The big man slid a flat pint bottle out of his hip pocket and handed it to my uncle. He said, "This your nephew Ed? Toots is gonna be disappointed; she wanted to know if he was gonna be with us. Maybe he's missing something, huh?"

"I wouldn't know," Uncle Ambrose said.

The big man laughed.

My uncle said, "Look, Hoagy, will you run along? I got to talk to Ed. His dad—my brother Wally—died last night."

"Jeez," said the big man. "I'm sorry, Am."

"That's all right. Leave me this bottle, will you, Hoagy? Say, you can run up the front right now if you want. The crowd's fair; I was getting a play."

"Sure, Am. Say, I'm goddam sorry about— Aw hell, you know what I mean."

The big man went out.

My uncle sat looking at me. I didn't say anything and neither did he for a minute or two. Then he said, "What's wrong, kid? What's eating you?"

"I don't know," I told him.

"Don't give me that," he said. "Look, Ed, I'm not as dumb as I look. I can tell you one thing. You haven't let your hair down. You haven't cried, have you? You're stiff as a board, and you can't take it that way; it'll do things to you. You're bitter."

"I'll be all right."

"No. What's eating you?"

He was still holding the flat pint bottle Hoagy had given

him. He hadn't taken the cap off. I looked at it and said, "Give me a drink, Uncle Ambrose."

He shook his head slowly. "That isn't the answer. If you drink, it ought to be because you want to. Not to run away from something. You've been running away ever since you found out, haven't you? Wally tried—Hell, Ed, you don't—"

"Listen," I said. "I don't want to get drunk. I just want one drink. It's something I got to do."

"Why?"

It was hard to say. I said, "I didn't know Pop. I found that out this morning. I thought I was too good for him. I thought he was a rumdum. He must have felt that. He must have felt I thought he was no good, and we never got to know each other, see?"

My uncle didn't say anything. He nodded slowly.

I went on. "I still hate the stuff. The taste of it, I mean. I like beer a little, but I hate the taste of whiskey. But I want to take a drink—to him. To make up, just a little bit, somehow. I know he'll never know, but I want to—to take a drink *to him*, like you do, sort of to— Oh, hell, I can't explain it any better than that."

My uncle said, "I'll be damned." He put the bottle down on the cot and went over to the trunk. He said, "I got some tin cups in here somewhere. For a cups-and-balls routine. It's almost illegal for a carney to drink out of anything but a bottle, but hell, kid, we got to drink that one together. I want to drink to Wally, too."

He came up with a set of three nested aluminum cups. He poured drinks—good generous ones, a third of a tumblerful—into two of them, and handed me one.

He said, "To Wally." I said, "To Pop," and we touched the

rims of the aluminum cups and downed it. It burned like the devil, but I managed not to choke on it.

Neither of us said anything for a minute, and then my uncle said, "I got to see Maury, the carney owner. Let him know I'm going."

He went out quick.

I sat there, with the awful taste of the raw whiskey in my mouth, but I wasn't thinking about that. I thought about Pop, and that Pop was dead and I'd never see him again. And suddenly I was bawling like hell. It wasn't the whiskey, because outside of the taste and the burn there isn't any effect for a while after you take a first drink. It was just that something let go inside me. I suppose my uncle knew it was coming, that way, and that's why he left me alone. He knew a guy my age wouldn't want to bawl in front of anyone.

By the time I was over crying, though, I began to feel the liquor. My head felt light, and I began to feel sick at my stomach.

Uncle Ambrose came back. He must have noticed my eyes were red, because he said, "You'll feel better now, Ed. You had that coming. You were tight like a drumhead. Now you look human."

I managed a grin. I said, "I guess I'm a bush-leaguer on drinking, though. I'm going to be sick, I think. Where's the can?"

"With a carney, it's a doniker. Other side of the lot. But hell, this is just a dirt lot. Go ahead and be sick. Or go outside, if you'd rather."

I went outside, around back of the tent, and got it over with.

When I came back, my uncle was through packing the suitcase. He said, "One drink oughtn't to have made you sick, kid, even if you aren't used to it. You been eating?"

"Gosh," I said, "not since supper last night. I never thought about it.

He laughed. "No wonder. Come on. We go to the chow top first; you put yourself outside a meal. I'll take the suitcase, and we hit for the station from there."

Uncle Ambrose ordered me a meal and waited until he saw me really start to eat it, then he said he'd be gone a little while again, and left me eating.

He came back just as I was finishing. He slid into the seat across the table and told me, "I just phoned the station. We can make the train that gets in Chi at six-thirty this evening. And I called Madge"—Madge is Mom's name—"and got the lowdown. Nothing new's come up, and the inquest's tomorrow afternoon. It's at Heiden's funeral parlors, on Wells Street. That's where—where he is now."

"Wouldn't—I thought he'd be taken to the morgue," I said.

My uncle shook his head. "Not in Chicago, Ed. The system's to take a body—unless it's somebody or something special—to the nearest private mortuary. City stands the bill, of course, unless relatives turn up and arrange for the mortician to handle things. A funeral, I mean."

"What if they don't turn up?"

"Potter's Field. Point is, they open an inquest right away to get down testimony while it's fresh. Then they adjourn it if they have to."

I nodded. I asked, "Was Mom mad because I sort of—well—ran off?"

"I don't think so. But she said the detective in charge of the case had wanted to talk to you, and was annoyed. She said she'd let him know you were on the way back."

"The hell with him," I said. "I can't tell him anything."

"Don't be like that, kid. We want him on our side."

"Our side?"

He looked at me strangely. "Why, sure, Ed," he said, "on our side. You're with me, aren't you?"

"You mean you're going to—to—"

"Hell, yes. That's why I had to fix things with Hoagy and Maury—he bought the carney this season but kept Hobart's name on it—so I could stay away as long as I had to. Hell, yes, kid. You don't think we're going to let some son of a bitch get away with killing your dad, do you?"

I said, "Can we do anything the cops can't?"

"They can put only limited time on it, unless they get hot leads. We got all the time in the world. That's one point. We got something they haven't got. We're the Hunters."

I got a tingling sensation when he said that, like a shock.

I thought, *we are the Hunters.* The name fits. We're going hunting in the dark alleys for a killer. The man who killed Pop.

Maybe it was screwy, but I believed him. We've got something the cops haven't got. We're Hunters. I was glad now I hadn't sent a telegram.

I said, "Okay. And we'll *get* the son of a bitch."

The twinkle was back in his eyes. But back of it was something—something deadly. In spite of that twinkle, he didn't look like a funny little fat man with a big black moustache any more. He looked like someone you wanted on your side when there was trouble.

When we got off the train in Chicago, Uncle Ambrose said, "We'll separate here for a while, kid. You go back home, make your peace with Madge and wait for the detective, if she says he's coming around. I'll phone you where I am."

"And after that?" I asked.

"If it's not too late, and you're not ready to turn in, maybe we can get together again. We might even figure something to do—I mean getting a start. You find out what you can from that detective. And from Madge."

"Okay," I said. "But why don't you come home with me now?"

He shook his head slowly. "The less Madge and I see of each other, in general, the better we'll get along. She was okay over the phone when I called from Janesville, but I don't want to crowd it, see?"

"Look," I said. "I don't want to stay there. Why can't I get a room, too? Near yours or maybe even a double. If we're going to be working together—"

"No, Ed. Not right away, anyway. I don't know how things are between you and Madge, but you got to live home—at the very least till after the funeral. It wouldn't look right or be right if you left now. See?"

"I guess so. I guess you're right."

"And if you left, and Madge didn't like it, she'd blame me and we'd both be in her doghouse and well—look, if we're going to work on the case we got to stay friendly with everyone connected with it. Get what I mean?"

I said, "Mom didn't do it, if that's what you mean. They scrapped once in a while, but she wouldn't have killed him."

"That isn't what I meant, no. I don't think she would have, either. But we got to have you staying at home, for a while. That's where your dad lived, see? We got to be able to trace this thing every way from the middle. Not just from the outside. You keep in with Madge, just like I want you to keep in with the detective, so you can ask 'em questions any time we find any questions need asking. We'll need every break we can get. Understand?"

Mom was there alone when I got home. Gardie was out somewhere; I didn't ask where she was. Mom was wearing a black dress that I didn't recognize. Her eyes were red, like she'd been crying plenty, and she didn't have on any make-up except a little lipstick that was a bit smeared at one corner of her mouth.

Her voice didn't sound like her at all. It was flat, sort of half-dead, without much inflection in it.

We were like strangers, somehow.

She said, "Hello, Ed," and I said, "Hello, Mom," and I went on in the living room and sat down and she came in and sat down too. I sat by the radio and fiddled with the dials without turning it on.

I said, "Mom, I'm sorry I—well, kind of ran out on you this morning. I should have stayed around." I was sorry, too, although I was glad I'd got Uncle Ambrose.

"That's all right, Ed," she told me. "I—I guess I understand why you wanted to get out. But how did you know about it? I mean, you weren't here when the cops came and—"

"I was on the stairs," I said. "I heard it. I—I didn't want to come in. Did you call the Elwood Press and tell them?"

She nodded. "We called from the undertaker's. I thought you'd gone to work alone, and we called to tell you. The foreman was nice about it. Said for you to take off as long as you wanted. To come back whenever you're ready. You—you are going back, aren't you, Ed?"

"I guess so," I said.

"It's a good trade. And W-Wally said you were getting along swell learning it. You ought to stick to it."

"I guess I will."

"Have you eaten, Ed? Can I get something for you?"

She was sure different. She'd never given much of a damn before whether I ate or not.

"I ate at Janesville," I said. "Uncle Ambrose went to a hotel. He said he'd phone and let us know where he took a room."

"He could have come here."

I didn't know what to say to that. I went back to fiddling with the radio dials, not looking at her. She looked so miserable I didn't want to look at her.

After awhile she said, "Listen, Ed—"

"Yes, Mom."

"I know you don't like me, much. Or Gardie. I know you'll want to go out on your own now. You're eighteen, and we're just step-relatives to you and—I don't blame you. But will you stay here awhile, first?"

"After awhile, we'll work it out. Gardie and I will find a smaller place, and I'll get a job. I want her to finish high school, like you did. But the rent's paid till the first of September, and we'll have to give a month's notice then and pay another month, and this place is too big for just us and—you see what I mean. If you can stay here that long—"

"All right," I said.

"It'll help out. We can get along till then, can't we, Ed?"

"Sure."

"Right after the funeral, I'll get a job. A waitress again, I guess. We can sell the furniture before we leave here. It's all paid for. Not worth much, but maybe we can get enough to almost cover the funeral cost."

I said, "You can sell it, but you don't need to worry about the funeral. The union mortuary benefit ought to cover that."

She looked puzzled, and I explained about it. Pop had been out of the trade for a few years, a bit back, and didn't have continuous membership long enough to draw the maximum, but there ought to be about five hundred coming from the international and the local together. I didn't know exactly, but it would be close to that.

She asked, "You're sure, Ed? That there *is* a benefit, I mean?"

"Positive," I said. "The I. T. U.'s a good union, all right. You can count on it. Maybe something from Elwood, too."

"Then I'm going down to Heiden's right now."

"What for, Mom?"

"I want Wally to have a good funeral, Ed. The best we can give him. I thought we'd have to go in debt for it, and maybe square off part of it with the furniture. I told him I thought about two hundred was all we could afford. I'm going to tell them to double that."

I said, "Pop wouldn't want you to spend it all on that. You should have some to start on. To get you and Gardie set up. And there'll be rent and expenses besides the funeral, and—well, I don't think you ought to do it."

She stood up. "I'm going to. A skimpy little funeral—"

I said, "It's day after tomorrow. You can change it tomorrow, after we know how much the mortuary benefit is. Wait till tomorrow morning, Mom."

She hesitated and then said, "Well, all right. Tomorrow morning won't be too late. I'm going to make some coffee, Ed. We'll have a cup; even if you're not hungry you can drink coffee."

"Sure," I said. "Thanks. Can I help?"

"You sit right here." She glanced at the clock. "The man from homicide that wants to talk to you—his name's Bassett—will be here at eight o'clock."

She turned in the doorway. She said, "And thanks, Ed, for—for deciding to stay, and everything. I thought maybe—"

There were tears running down her face.

I felt almost like crying myself. I felt like a damn fool sitting there not saying anything. But I couldn't think of what to say.

I said, "Aw, Mom—"

I wished I could put my arms around her and try to comfort her, but you can't do something like that all of a sudden when you never have. Not in ten years.

She went on out into the kitchen and I heard the click of the light switch. I felt all mixed up again inside.

CHAPTER 3

BASSETT CAME AT EIGHT O'CLOCK. I was drinking coffee with Mom and she put out another cup, and he sat across the table from me. He didn't look like a police detective. He wasn't big; just average height, my height, and no heavier than I am, either. He had faded reddish hair and faded freckles. His eyes looked tired behind shell-rimmed glasses.

But he was nice, and he was friendly. He wasn't like a copper at all.

Instead of asking a flock of questions, he just asked, "Well, what happened to you, kid?" and then listened while I told him all about it from the time I'd knocked on the door of their room and Pop hadn't answered. Only thing I didn't mention was Mom's being dressed all but her shoes. That couldn't have anything to do with it, and wasn't any of his business. Wherever she'd gone, it didn't matter any now.

When I'd finished, he sat there, not saying anything at all, just sipping at his coffee. I didn't say anything, and neither did Mom. The phone rang, and I said it was probably for me, and went into the living room to answer it.

It was Uncle Ambrose. He had a room at the Wacker on North Clark Street, only a few blocks away.

"Swell," I said. "Why don't you come on around, right now? Mr. Bassett—the detective—is here."

"Like to," he said. "Is it okay with Madge, you think?"

"Sure. It's okay. Make it right away."

I went back to the kitchen and told them he was coming.

"You say he's a carney?" Bassett asked.

I nodded. "He's a swell guy," I said. "Look, Mr. Bassett, mind if I ask you something, straight?"

"Shoot, kid."

"What are the chances of the pol—of you finding the guy who did it? Kind of slim, aren't they?"

"Kind of," he said. "There's almost nothing to go on, see? A guy who pulls a job like that takes a plenty big chance of getting caught—at the time he does it. He's got to worry a squad car might go by—and they flash their spots down alleys in that district. He's got to watch out for the beat cop. The guy he tackles just might show fight and get the best of him.

"But once he's done it, see, and got away in the clear, he's pretty safe. If he keeps his lip buttoned—well, there's a chance in a thousand, ten thousand maybe, that he's not got away with it."

I said, "On a case like this"—somehow I wanted to keep it general; I didn't want to talk about Pop—"just what would that one chance be?"

"Could be a lot of things. Maybe he takes a watch off the man he kills. We turn over the number to the pawnshop detail and maybe later it turns up in a pawnshop and we can trace it back."

"Pop wouldn't have had his watch," I said. "He left it to be repaired a few days ago."

"Yeah. Well, another way. He might have been followed.

I mean, he might have flashed money in a tavern, so when he leaves, somebody leaves just after him. Somebody in the tavern might remember that and might give us a description, or even know the guy. See?"

I nodded. "You know where he was last night?"

"On Clark Street, first. Stopped in at least two taverns there; could be more. Had only a couple beers in each. He was alone. Then we picked up the last place he was; we're fairly sure it was the last place. Out west on Chicago Avenue, other side of Orleans. He was alone there too, and nobody left just after he did."

I asked, "How do you know that was the last place?"

"He bought some bottle beer there to take home. Besides, that was around one o'clock, and he was found at about two. And then where he was found was between here and there, like he'd started home. Then there aren't any taverns to speak of between here and there, along that route. The couple there are, we checked damn thoroughly. He could've stopped in one of them, but—well, what with the bottle beer and the time and everything, it's odds on he didn't."

"Where—where *was* he found?"

"Alley between Orleans and Franklin, two and a half blocks south of Chicago Avenue."

"Between Huron and Erie?"

He nodded.

I said, "Then he must have walked south on Orleans and cut through the alley toward Franklin. But—gosh, in *that* neighborhood, why'd he want to go through an alley?"

Bassett said, "Two answers to that. One is—he'd been drinking a lot of beer. Far as we know, he hadn't drunk much else, and he'd been out and around from nine o'clock to one. A guy starting home with a skinful of beer might easy want to cut through an alley, although like you say, it's no neighborhood to do it in."

"What's the other answer?"

"That he didn't cut through the alley at all. He was near the Franklin end. So he could have walked over Chicago to Franklin and south on Franklin. He's stuck up at the mouth of the alley, and the stick-up man, or men, take him into the alley, roll him there and then slug him. Those streets are pretty deserted that time in the morning. There've been plenty of holdups there under the el on Franklin."

I nodded thoughtfully. This Bassett didn't look like a detective, but he wasn't a dumb cluck at all. Either of the things he'd said could have happened. It had to have been one way or the other, and the odds looked about even.

And they looked pretty slim for getting the guy who did it. Like he said, about a thousand to one against.

Could be, I thought, he's smarter than Uncle Ambrose on things like this. He was smart enough to have traced Pop pretty well, and that was no cinch in a district like this. On Clark Street and on Chicago Avenue they don't like coppers. Even the most of them who are inside the law.

When Uncle Ambrose came, Mom let him in. They talked a few minutes out in the hall and I could hear their voices but I couldn't tell what they were saying. When they came in the kitchen they were friendly. Mom poured another cup of coffee.

Bassett shook hands with him and they seemed to take to one another right away. Bassett started asking him questions, just a few. He didn't ask him whether I'd been in Janesville; he asked, quite casually, what train I'd come on and how service was coming back and some things like that. And little points he could check with the story I'd told him so he'd know if I'd been telling him the truth.

A smart duck, I thought again.

But I didn't know the half of it until Uncle Ambrose started asking a few questions about the investigation. Bassett answered the first couple and then one corner of his mouth went up a little.

He said, "Ask the kid here. I gave him the whole story, such as it is. You two are going at it together. I wish you luck."

My uncle looked at me, his eyebrows up just a trifle. Bassett wasn't watching me, so I shook my head a little to let him know I hadn't blabbed to the detective. A smart duck. I don't know how he figured that angle so quickly.

Gardie came in and got reintroduced to Uncle Ambrose. Mom had sent her out to a movie, and I guess she'd really gone to one or she wouldn't have been home so early.

I got a kick out of the way Uncle Ambrose patted her on the head and treated her like a kid. Gardie didn't like it; I could tell that. Five minutes of old-home-week and she went off to her room.

Uncle Ambrose grinned at me.

The coffee was cold and Mom started to get some fresh, but Uncle Ambrose said, "Let's go down and have a drink instead. What say, Bassett?"

The detective shrugged. "Okay by me. I'm off duty now."

Mom shook her head. "You two go," she told them.

I dealt myself in, said I was thirsty and wanted some Seven-Up or a coke. Uncle Ambrose said, "Sure," and Mom didn't squawk, so I went downstairs with them.

We went to a place on Grand Avenue. Bassett said it was a

quiet place where we could talk. It was quiet all right; we were almost the only ones in there.

We took a booth and ordered two beers and a Coca-Cola. Bassett said he had to phone somebody and went back to the phone booth.

I said, "He's a nice guy. I kind of like him."

My uncle nodded slowly. He said, "He's not dumb and he's not honest and he's not a louse. He's just what the doctor ordered."

"Huh? How do you know he's not honest?" I wasn't being naïve; I know plenty of coppers aren't; I just wondered how Uncle Ambrose could be so sure so quick—or if he was just talking through his hat.

"Just looking at him," he said. "I don't know how, but I know. I used to run a mitt-camp with the carney, Ed. It's a racket, sure, but you get so you can size people up."

I remembered something I'd read. "Lombroso has been dis—"

"Nuts to Lombroso. It isn't the shapes of their faces. It's something you feel. You can do it with your eyes shut. I don't know how. But this red-headed copper—we're going to buy him."

He took out his wallet, and holding it under the table so the couple of men at the bar, up front, couldn't see what he was doing, he took a bill out of it and then put it back in his hip pocket. I got a look at the bill, though, as he folded it twice and palmed it. It was a hundred bucks.

I felt a little scared. I couldn't see why he would need to bribe Bassett at all, and I was afraid he was wrong, and offering it would start trouble.

Bassett came back and sat down.

My uncle said, "Look, Bassett, I know what you're up against on a case like this. But Wally was my brother, see, and I want to see the guy who killed him sent up. I want to see him fry."

Bassett said, "We'll do our best."

"I know you will. But they won't allow you too much time on it, and you know that. I want to help any way I can. There's one way I know of. I mean, there's times putting out a few bucks here and there will get a song out of somebody who won't sing otherwise. You know what I mean."

"I know what you mean. Yeah, sometimes it helps."

My uncle held out his hand, palm down. He said, "Put this in your pocket, in case you get a chance to use it where it might get us something. It's off the record."

Bassett took the bill. I saw him glance at the corner of it under the table, and then he put it in his pocket. His face didn't change. He didn't say anything.

We ordered another round of drinks, or they did. I still had half my coke left.

Bassett's eyes, behind the shell-rimmed glasses, looked a little more tired, a little more veiled. He said, "What I gave the kid was straight. We don't know a damn thing more. Two stops on Clark Street; stayed maybe half an hour in each. That one last stop on Grand Avenue; where he bought the beer. Ten gets you one that was the last stop he made. If we could get anything, it ought to be there. But there wasn't anything to get."

"What about the rest of the time?" my uncle asked.

Bassett shrugged. "There are two kind of drinkers. One holes in someplace and stays put to do his drinking. The other kind ambles. Wallace Hunter was the ambling kind, that evening anyway. He was out four hours and stuck around about half an hour—long enough to drink two-three beers in each of the three places we've put him. If that's the average, he probably stopped in six or seven places—you got to allow some time for the walking."

"He drank only beer?"

"Mostly, anyway. One place, the bartender wasn't sure what he drank. And on Chicago Avenue, he had one shot with his last beer, then bought the bottles to go. Kaufman's place. Kaufman was behind the bar. Said he seemed a little tight, quiet drunk, but not staggering or anything. In control."

"Who's Kaufman? I mean, outside of being a tavern owner."

"Nobody much. I don't know how straight he is, but we haven't got anything on him if he isn't. I checked with the boys at the Chicago Avenue station on that. As far as they know, his nose is clean."

"You talked to him. Is it?"

Bassett said, "He could do with a handkerchief. But I think he's clean on this. He came up with identifying your brother's picture after I'd jogged him a little. Used the same line on him as the others; I mean, told 'em we knew he was there and was only interested in getting the time he left. First he said he never saw him. I said we had proof he'd been in there, just wanted to know when, and it wouldn't get him in any trouble. So he got some glasses out of a drawer and looked again, and then kicked in."

"All the way?"

"I think so," Bassett said. "You'll get a look at him and a listen to him tomorrow, at the inquest."

"Swell," my uncle told me. "Look, you don't know me at the inquest. Nobody does. I just sit at the back, and nobody knows who I am. They won't want me to testify anyway."

Bassett's eyes unveiled a little, just a little. He asked, "You think you might want to run one?"

"I think maybe," my uncle said.

They seemed to understand one another. They knew what they were talking about. I didn't.

Like when Hoagy, the big man, had been talking to my uncle about the blow being sloughed. Only that was carney talk; at least I knew why I didn't understand it. This was different; they were talking words I knew, but it still didn't make sense.

I didn't care.

Bassett said, "One angle's out. No insurance."

That did make sense to me. I said, "Mom didn't do it."

Bassett looked at me, and I wondered if I liked him as much as I'd thought.

Uncle Ambrose said, "The kid's right. Madge is—" He stopped himself. "She wouldn't have killed Wally."

"You can't tell with women. My God, I've known cases—"

"Sure, a million cases. But Madge didn't kill him. Look, she might have waited till he got home and gone for him with a butcher knife or something. But this wasn't like that. She wouldn't have followed him into an alley and blackj—Say, *was* it a blackjack?"

"Nope. Something harder."

"Such as?"

"Almost anything heavy enough to swing and without a point or sharp edge on the side that hit. A club, a piece of pipe, an empty bottle, a—almost anything."

A blunt instrument, I thought. That's the way the papers would describe it, if the papers would print it.

I watched a cockroach that was crawling across the floor away from the bar. It was one of the big black kind, and it moved in hitches, scurrying a little and then stopping still. It would run for about ten inches, stop a second, then another ten inches.

One of the men at the bar was watching it. He walked toward it and it scurried out from under his foot just in time.

The second time it wasn't so lucky. There was a crunching sound.

"Look," Bassett was saying, "I got to get home. I just phoned there and my wife is kind of sick. Nothing serious, but she wanted me to bring some medicine. See you at the inquest tomorrow."

"Okay," said my uncle. "We can't talk there, though, like I said. How about meeting afterwards here?"

"Fine. So long. So long, kid."

He left.

I thought, a hundred bucks is a lot of money. I was glad I hadn't a job where people might offer me a hundred bucks for doing something I shouldn't do.

Not that, come to think of it, he was being paid for doing anything really wrong. Just for being on our side; for levelling with us. For giving us the straight dope on everything. That was all right; it was only the taking money for it that was wrong. But he had a sick wife.

And then I thought, my uncle didn't know he had a sick wife. But my uncle knew he'd take the hundred.

My uncle said, "It's a good investment."

"Maybe," I said. "But if he's dishonest, how do you know he'll play straight with you? He can give you nothing for that hundred dollars. And that's a lot of money."

He said, "Sometimes a dime is a lot of money. Sometimes a hundred isn't. I think we'll get our money's worth. Look, kid, how about making the rounds? I mean, looking over the places he stopped. One thing I want to know. You feel up to it?"

"Sure," I said. "I can't sleep anyway. And it's only eleven."

He looked me over. He said, "You can pass for twenty-one, I think. If anyone asks, I'm your father and they ought to take my word for it. We can both show identification with the same name. Only we don't want to."

"You mean we don't want them to know who we are?"

"That's it. Anyplace we go in, we order a beer apiece. I drink mine fast and you just sip yours. Then we get the glasses mixed, see? That way—"

"A little beer won't hurt me," I said. "I'm eighteen, damn it."

"A little beer won't hurt you. That's all you're going to get. We change glasses. See?"

I nodded. No use arguing, especially when he was right.

We walked over Grand to Clark and started north. We stopped on the corner of Ontario.

"This is sort of where he started," I said. "I mean, he would have come over on Ontario from Wells, and started north."

I stood there, looking down Ontario, feeling almost that I would see him coming.

It was very silly. I thought, he's lying on a slab at Heiden's. They've taken out his blood and filled him with embalming fluid. They'd have done that quick because the weather is so hot.

He isn't Pop any more. Pop had never minded hot weather. Cold got him down; he hated to go out in cold weather, even for a block or two. But hot weather he didn't mind.

Uncle Ambrose said, "The Beer Barrel and the Cold Spot, those are the two places, weren't they?"

I said, "I guess Bassett said that when I wasn't listening. I don't know."

"Wasn't listening?"

"I was watching a cockroach," I said.

He didn't say anything. We started walking, watching the names of the places we went past. The taverns average three or four to a block on North Clark Street from the Loop north to Bughouse Square. The poor man's Broadway.

We came to the Cold Spot just north of Huron. We went in and stood at the bar. The Greek behind the bar hardly looked at me.

There were only a few men along the bar, and no women. A drunk was asleep at a table near the back. We stayed only for the one beer apiece, Uncle Ambrose drinking most of mine.

We did the same at the Beer Barrel, which turned up on the other side of the street, near Chicago. It was the same kind of place, a little bigger, a few more people, two bartenders instead of one and three drunks asleep at tables instead of one.

There was no one near us at the bar, so we could talk freely.

I said, "Aren't you going to try to pump them? To find out what he was doing, or something?"

He shook his head.

I wanted to know, "What *were* we trying to find out?"

"What he was doing. What he was looking for."

I thought it over. It didn't make any sense that we could find that out without asking any questions.

My uncle said, "Come on, I'll show you."

We went out and walked back half a block the way we had come and went in another place.

"I get it," I told him. "I see what you mean."

I'd been kind of dumb. This was different. There was music, if you could call it that. And almost as many women as men. Faded women mostly. A few of them were young. Most of them were drunk.

They weren't percentage girls. Maybe a few of them, I decided, were prostitutes, but not many. They were just women.

We had our one beer apiece again.

I thought, I'm glad Pop didn't come here, places like this, instead of the Beer Barrel and the Cold Spot. He'd been out drinking. Just drinking.

We went north again and crossed back to the west side of the street and turned the corner at Chicago Avenue.

We passed the police station. We crossed LaSalle and then Wells. He could have turned south here, I thought. It would have been about half-past twelve when he came this way.

Last night, I thought. Only last night, he came this way. Probably walking on the same side of the street we were on. Only last night, and about at this time. It must be almost twelve-thirty right now, I thought.

We walked under the el at Franklin.

A train roared by overhead and it shook the night. Funny that the el trains are so loud at night. In our flat on Wells, a block from the el, I can hear every one at night, if I'm awake. Or early in the morning when I first get up or am still lying in bed. The rest of the time you can't hear them.

We walked on, as far as the corner of Orleans Street. We stopped there. Across the way was a Topaz Beer sign. It was on the north side of Chicago Avenue, two doors past the corner. It would be Kaufman's place. It would have to be, because it was the only tavern in the block.

Pop's last stop.

I asked, "Aren't we going over there?"

My uncle shook his head slowly.

We stood there maybe five minutes, doing nothing, not even talking. I didn't ask him why we weren't going over to Kaufman's.

Then he said, "Well, kid—?"

I said, "Sure."

We turned around and started walking south on Orleans.

We were going there now. We were going to the alley.

CHAPTER 4

THE ALLEY was just an alley. At the Orleans end there was a parking lot at one side and a candy factory at the other. There was a big loading platform alongside the candy factory.

The alley was paved with rough red brick and there were no curbs.

There was a street light, one of the smaller size they use in the middle of a block, opposite the Orleans end.

Down at the Franklin end, under the elevated, there was another such light, right at the left of the mouth of the alley. It wasn't particularly dark. You could stand at the Orleans end and look through it.

It was dim down in the middle of the alley, but you could see through it, and if anyone was in there you could see him silhouetted against the Franklin end.

There wasn't anyone in there now.

Down in the middle of the alley were the backs of flat buildings, ramshackle old ones, that fronted on Huron and on Erie. The ones on the Erie side had wooden back porches with railings, and wooden steps that led up to the back doors of the flats. The ones on the Huron side were flat and flush with the alley.

Uncle Ambrose said, "If he came this way, it must have been

somebody following him. He could have seen anyone waiting in the alley."

I pointed up at the porches. I said, "Somebody up on one of them. A man staggers through the alley below them. They go down the steps, getting down just after he passes, catch up with him near the other end of the alley, and—"

"Could be, kid. Not likely. If they were on the porch, then they live there. A guy doesn't do something like that in his own back alley. Not that close to home. And I doubt if he was staggering drunk. 'Course you got to discount how sober a bartender says a guy is when he leaves the place. They don't want to get themselves in trouble."

"It could have been that way," I said. "Not likely, but it could have been."

"Sure. We'll look into it. We'll talk to everybody lives in those flats. We're not passing up off chances; I didn't mean that when I said it wasn't likely."

We were talking softly, like you do in an alley at night. We were past the middle of the alley, past the flats. We were at the back of the buildings that fronted on Franklin Street. On both sides they were three-story bricks, with stores on the bottom floor and flats above.

My uncle stopped and bent down. He said, "Beer-bottle glass. This is where it happened."

I got a funny feeling, almost a dizziness. This is where it happened. Right where I'm standing now. This is where it happened.

I didn't want to think about it, that way, so I bent down and started looking, too. It was amber glass, all right, and over an area of a few yards there was enough of it to have come from two or three bottles.

It wouldn't be just like it fell, of course. It would have been kicked around by people walking through the alley, trucks driving through. It was broken finer now, and scattered more. But right around here, the center of the area where the glass was, would be where the bottles were dropped.

My uncle said, "Here's a piece with part of a label. We can see if it's the brand Kaufman sells."

I took it and walked out under the street light at the end of the alley. I said, "It's part of a Topaz label. I've seen thousands of 'em on beer Pop's brought home. Kaufman has a Topaz sign, but it's an awful common beer around here. It wouldn't prove it for sure."

He came over and we stood looking both ways on Franklin Street. An el train went by almost right over our heads. A long one, it must have been a North Shore train. It sounded as loud as the end of the world.

A noise loud enough, I thought, to cover revolver shots—let alone the noise a man would make falling, even with beer bottles. That might have been why it happened here, near this end of the alley, instead of back in the middle where it was darker. Noise counted, too, along with darkness. When they got here, the killer closing up behind Pop, the el had come by. Even if Pop had yelled for help, the noise of the el would have made it a whisper.

I looked at the store fronts on either side of the alley. One was a plumbing supplies shop. The other was vacant. It seemed to have been vacant a long time; the glass was too dirty to see through.

My uncle said, "Well, Ed."

"Sure. I guess this is—is all we can do tonight."

We walked down Franklin to Erie and across to Wells.

My uncle said, "I just figured what's wrong with me. I'm hungry as hell. I haven't eaten since noon and you haven't eaten since about two o'clock. Let's go over to Clark for some grub."

We went to an all-night barbecue place.

I wasn't hungry until I took a bite out of a pork barbecue sandwich, and then I gobbled it down, the French fries and the slaw too. We each ordered a second one.

My uncle asked, while we waited, "Ed, what are you heading for?"

"What do you mean?"

He said, "I mean what are you going to do with yourself? During the next fifty-odd years."

The answer was so obvious I had to think it over. I said, "Nothing much, I guess. I'm an apprentice printer. I can take up linotype when I'm a little farther on my apprenticeship. Or I can be a hand-man. Printing's a good trade."

"I suppose it is. Going to stay in Chicago?"

"I haven't thought about it," I told him. "I'm not going to leave right away. After I finish my apprenticeship, I'm a journeyman. I can work anywhere."

He said, "A trade's a good thing. But get the trade, don't let it get you. The same with— Oh, hell, I'm not Dutch. I'm talking like a Dutch uncle."

He grinned. He'd been going to say, the same with women. He knew that I knew it and so he didn't have to say it. I was glad he gave me credit for that much sense.

He asked instead, "What do you dream, Ed?"

I looked at him; he was serious. I asked, "Is this the mitt-camp lay? Or are you psychoanalyzing me?"

"It's the same difference."

I said, "This morning I dreamed I was reaching through a hockshop window to pick up a trombone. Gardie came skipping rope along the sidewalk and I woke up before I got the trombone. Now I suppose you know all about me, huh?"

He chuckled. "That would be shooting a sitting duck, Ed. Two ducks with one bullet. Watch out for one of those ducks. You know which one I mean."

"I guess I do."

"She's poison, kid, for a guy like you. Just like Madge was— Skip it. What's about the tram? Ever play one?"

"Not to speak of. In sophomore year at high I borrowed one of the school board's. I was going to learn so I could get in the band. But some of the neighbors squawked, and I guess it did make a hell of a noise. When you live in a flat— Mom didn't like it, either."

The guy behind the counter brought our second sandwiches. I wasn't so hungry now. With the stuff on the side, it looked awfully big. I ate a few of the French fries first.

Then I lifted the lid off the barbecue sandwich and tilted the ketchup bottle and let it gurgle on thick.

It looked like—

I smacked down the lid of the sandwich and tried to think away from what it looked like. But I was back in the alley. I didn't even know if there'd been blood; maybe there hadn't. You can hit to kill without drawing blood.

But I thought of Pop's head matted with blood and a blot of blood there on the rough brick of the alley last night—now soaked in, worn off or washed away. Would they have washed it away? Hell, there probably hadn't been any blood.

But the thought of that sandwich was making me sick. Unless I could get my mind off it. I closed my eyes and was repeating the first nonsense that came into my mind to keep from thinking. It was *one, two, three, O'Leary; four, five, six, O'Leary*—

After a few seconds I knew I'd won and I wasn't going to be sick. But I looked around at Uncle Ambrose and kept my eyes off the counter.

I said, "Say, maybe Mom's waiting up for me. We never thought to tell her we'd be late. It's after one."

He said, "My God, I forgot it too. Golly, I hope she isn't. You better get home fast."

I told him I didn't want the rest of my second barbecue anyway, and he'd almost finished his. We parted right outside; he went north to the Wacker and I hurried home to Wells Street.

Mom had left a light on for me in the inner hall, but she hadn't waited up. The door of her room was dark. I was glad. I didn't want to have to explain and apologize, and if she'd been waiting up, worried, she might have blamed Uncle Ambrose.

I got to bed quickly and quietly. I must have gone to sleep the first instant I closed my eyes.

When I woke up, something was funny in the room. Different. It was morning as usual and again the room was hot and close. It took me a minute or two, lying there, to realize that the difference was that my alarm clock wasn't ticking. I hadn't wound or set it.

I don't know why it mattered much what time it was, but I wanted to know. I got up and walked out to look at the kitchen clock. It was one minute after seven.

Funny, I thought; I waked up at just the usual time. Without even a clock running in my room.

Nobody else was awake. Gardie's door was open and her pajama tops were off again. I hurried past.

I set and wound my alarm clock and lay down again. I might as well sleep another hour or two, I thought, if I can. But I couldn't go back to sleep; I couldn't even get sleepy.

The flat was awfully quiet. There didn't seem to be much noise even outside this morning, except when an el car went by on Franklin every few minutes.

The ticking of the clock got louder and louder.

This morning I don't have to wake Pop, I thought. I'll never wake him again. Nobody will.

I got up and dressed.

On my way through to the kitchen I stopped in the doorway of Gardie's room and looked in. I thought, she wants me to look; I want to look, so why shouldn't I? I knew the answer damn well.

Maybe I was looking for a counter-irritant for the cold feeling about not having to wake up Pop. Maybe a cold feeling and a hot one ought to cancel out. They didn't, exactly, but after half a minute I got disgusted with myself and went on out to the kitchen.

I made coffee and sat drinking it. I wondered what I was going to do to fill in the morning. Uncle Ambrose would sleep late; being with a carney he'd be used to sleeping late. Anyway there wasn't much to do about the investigation until after the inquest. And then, until after the funeral.

Besides, in the light of morning now, it seemed a bit silly. A fat little man with a moustache and a wet-behind-the-ears kid thinking they could find, out of all Chicago, the heister who had got away with a job.

I thought about the homicide man with the faded red hair and the tired eyes. We'd bought him for a hundred dollars, or

Uncle Ambrose thought we had. He'd been partly right any-how; Bassett had taken the money.

I heard bare feet padding, and Gardie came out into the kitchen in her pajamas. The tops, too. The toenails of her bare feet were painted.

She said, "Morning, Eddie. Cup coffee?"

She yawned and then stretched like a sleek kitten. Her claws were in.

I got another cup and poured, and she sat down across the table.

She said, "Gee, the inquest's today." She sounded excited about it. Like she would say, "Gee, the football game's today."

I said, "I wonder if they'll want me to testify. I don't know to what."

"No, Eddie, I don't think so. Just Mom and me, they said."

"Why you?"

"Identification. I was the one really identified him first. Mom almost fainted again at the parlors, at Heiden's. They didn't want her to faint, so I said I'd look. Later when she was a little calmer, after the detective, Mr. Bassett, had talked to her, she wanted to look too, and they let her."

I asked, "How did they find out who he was? I mean, he couldn't have had identification left on him or they'd have been up here in the middle of the night, after they found him."

"Bobby knew him. Bobby Reinhart."

"Who's Bobby Reinhart?"

"He works for Mr. Heiden. He's learning the undertaking business. I've gone out with him a few times. He knew Pop by sight. He came to work at seven, and told them right away who it was, as soon as he went in the—the morgue room."

"Oh," I said. I placed the guy now. A slick-looking little punk, about sixteen or seventeen. He greased his hair and had always worn his best clothes to school. He thought he was a woman-killer and pretty hot stuff.

It made me a little sick to think of him maybe helping work on Pop's body.

We finished the coffee, and Gardie rinsed out the cups and then went back to her room to dress. I heard Mom getting up.

I went in the living room and picked up a magazine. It was starting to rain outside, a slow steady drizzle.

It was a detective magazine. I started a story and it was about a rich man who was found dead in his hotel suite, with a noose of yellow silk rope around his neck, but he'd been poisoned. There were lots of suspects, all with motives. His secretary at whom he'd been making passes, a nephew who inherited, a racketeer who owed him money, the secretary's fiancé. In the third chapter they'd just about pinned it on the racketeer and then *he's* murdered. There's a yellow silk cord around his neck and he's been strangled, but not with the silk cord.

I put down the book. Nuts, I thought, murder isn't like that. Murder is like this.

For some reason, I got to remembering the time Pop took me to the aquarium. I don't know how I remembered that; I was only about six years old then, or maybe five. My mother had been alive then, but she hadn't gone with us. I remember Pop and I laughing a lot together at the expressions on the faces of some of the fishes, the surprised astonished look on the faces of some of them that had round open mouths.

Now that I thought about it, Pop had laughed a lot in those days.

Gardie told Mom she was going to a girl friend's house and would be back by noon.

It rained all morning.

At the inquest, it seemed you mostly sat around and waited for it to start. It was in the main hall at Heiden's mortuary. There hadn't been any sign out "Inquest Today" but word must have got around, because there were quite a few people there. There were seats for about forty and they were all taken.

Uncle Ambrose was there, in the back row on one side. He'd tipped me a wink and then pretended not to know me. I let myself get separated from Mom and Gardie and took a seat near the back on the other side of the room.

A little man with gold-rimmed glasses was fussing around, up front. He was the deputy coroner in charge. I found out later his name was Wheeler. He looked hot and fussy and annoyed, and in a hurry to get things started and get them over with.

Bassett was there, and other cops, one in uniform, the others not. There was a man with a long thin nose who looked like a professional gambler.

There were six men in chairs lined up along one side of the front of the hall.

Finally, whatever was holding up things must have been settled. The deputy coroner rapped with a gavel and things quieted down. He wanted to know if there was any objection to any of the six men who had been chosen as jurors. There wasn't. He wanted to know, of them, whether they had known a man named Wallace Hunter, whether they knew the circumstances of his death or had discussed the case with anyone, whether there was any reason why they couldn't render a fair and impartial verdict on the evidence they would hear. He got negatives and headshakes on all counts.

Then he took the six of them into the morgue to view the body of the deceased, and then to be sworn.

It was very formal, in an informal sort of way.

It was corny. It was like a bad movie.

When that was all out of the way, he wanted to know if there was a member of the family of the deceased present. Mom got up and went forward. She held up her right hand and mumbled something back when something was mumbled at her.

Her name, her address, her occupation, her relation to the deceased. She had seen the body and identified it as that of her husband.

A lot of questions about Pop; his occupation, place of employment, residence, how long he'd lived there and all that sort of thing.

"When did you last see your husband alive, Mrs. Hunter?"

"Thursday night, somewhere about nine o'clock. When he went out."

"Did he say where he was going?"

"N-no. He just said he was going down for a glass of beer. I figured Clark Street."

"Did he go out like that often, alone?"

"Well—yes."

"How often?"

"Once or twice a week."

"And usually stayed out—how late?"

"Around midnight usually. Sometimes later. One or two o'clock."

"How much money did he have with him Thursday night?"

"I don't know exactly. Twenty or thirty dollars. Wednesday was payday."

"You can't say any closer than that?"

"No. He gave me twenty-five dollars Wednesday night. That was for groceries and—and household expenses. He always kept the rest. He paid rent and gas and light bills and things like that."

"He had no enemies that you know of, Mrs. Hunter?"

"No, none at all."

"Think carefully. You know of no one who would—would have cause to hate him?"

Mom said, "No. Nobody at all."

"Nor anyone who would benefit financially from his death?"

"How do you mean?"

"I mean, did he have any money, did he have an interest in any business or venture?"

"No."

"Did he carry any insurance? Or was any insurance carried on him?"

"No. He suggested it once. I said no, that we ought to put the money that would go for premiums in the bank instead. Only we didn't."

"Thursday night, Mrs. Hunter, did you wait up for him?"

"I did, yes, for a while. Then I decided he was going to be late and I went to sleep."

"When your husband had been drinking, Mrs. Hunter, would you say he was—well, careless about taking chances such as walking down alleys or in dangerous neighborhoods, things like that?"

"I'm afraid he was, yes. He was held up before, twice. The last time a year ago."

"But he wasn't injured? He didn't attempt to defend himself?"

"No. He was just held up."

I listened closely now. That was news to me. Nobody had told me Pop had been held up before, not even once. Then something fitted. A year ago he'd said he'd lost his wallet; he'd had to get a new social security card and union card. Probably he'd just figured it was none of my business how he'd lost it.

The deputy coroner was asking if any of the police present wanted to ask any further questions. Nobody did, and he told Mom she could go back to her seat.

He said, "I understand we have a further identification. Miss Hildegarde Hunter has also identified the deceased. Is she present?"

Gardie got up and went through the rigmarole. She sat down in the chair and crossed her legs. She didn't have to adjust her skirt; it was short enough already.

They didn't ask her anything except about having identified Pop. You could tell she was disappointed when she went back to her seat beside Mom.

They put one of the plain-clothes men on the stand next. He was a squad-car cop. He and his partner had found the body.

They'd been driving south, just cruising slowly, on Franklin Street under the el at two o'clock and the alley was dark there and they'd flashed their spotlight in it and seen him lying there.

"He was dead when you reached him?"

"Yes. Been dead about an hour maybe."

"You looked for identification?"

"Yes. He didn't have any wallet or watch or anything. He'd been cleaned. There was some change in his pocket. Sixty-five cents."

"It was dark enough back where he lay that anyone walking by would not have seen him?"

"I guess not. There's a street light on Franklin at that end of the alley, but it was out. We reported that too, afterward, and they put in a new bulb. Or said they were going to."

"Was there any indication of a struggle?"

"Well, his face was scratched, but that could have been from falling. He fell face forward when he was hit."

"You don't know that," said the coroner, sharply.

"You mean, he was lying on his face when you found him?"

"Yeah. And there was broken glass from several beer bottles and the spot smelled of beer. The alley and his clothes were wet with it. He must have been carrying—Oh, all right, that's a deduction again. There was beer and beer-bottle glass around."

"Was the deceased wearing a hat?"

"There was one laying by him. A hard straw hat. What they call a sailor straw. It wasn't crushed; it couldn't have been on him when he was hit. That, and the way he was laying makes me think he was slugged from behind. The heister came up on him, knocked off his hat with one hand and swung the billy with the other, like. You can't take off a guy's hat to slug him from the front without him knowing it and he'd put up a—"

"Please confine yourself to the facts, Mr. Horvath."

"Okay—what *was* the question, now?"

"Was the deceased wearing a hat? That was the question."

"No, he wasn't wearing one. There was one laying by him."

"Thank you, Mr. Horvath. That will be all."

The cop got down from the witness chair. I thought, we were figuring things wrong last night, because we figured on that street light. It was off at the time. It would have been plenty dark at the Franklin end of the alley.

The deputy coroner was looking at his notes again. He said, "Is there a Mr. Kaufman present?"

A short, heavy man shuffled forward. He wore glasses with thick lenses and behind them his eyes looked hooded.

His name, he testified, was George Kaufman. He owned and ran the tavern on Chicago Avenue known as Kaufman's Place.

Yes, Wallace Hunter, the deceased, had been in his tavern Thursday night. He'd been there half an hour—not much longer than that anyhow—and then had left, saying he was going home. In Kaufman's place he'd had one shot and two-three beers. In answer to a question, Mr. Kaufman admitted it might have been three or four beers, but not more than that. He was sure about it being only one shot.

"He came in alone?"

"Yeah. He came in alone. And left alone."

"Did he say he was going home when he left?"

"Yeah. He was standing at the bar. He said something about going home, I don't remember the words. And he bought four bottles to take out. Paid for 'em and left."

"You knew him? He'd been in before?"

"A few times. I knew him by sight. I didn't know his name until they showed me his picture and told me."

"How many others were in your tavern at the time?"

"Two guys together were there, when he came in. They were getting ready to leave then, and they left. Nobody else came in."

"You mean he was the only customer?"

"Most of the time he was there, yeah. It was a dull evening. I closed early. A little after he left."

"How long after?"

"I started to clean up the place for closing then. It was about twenty minutes before I got it closed. Maybe thirty."

"Did you see how much money he had?"

"He broke a five. He took it out of his wallet, but I didn't see inside his wallet when he took it out or put the singles back. I don't know how much more he had."

"The two men who left when he came. Do you know them?"

"A little. One of 'em runs a delicatessen on Wells Street. He's Jewish; I don't know his name. The other guy comes in with him."

"Was the deceased in an intoxicated condition, would you say?"

"He'd been drinking. He showed it, but I wouldn't say he was drunk."

"He could walk straight?"

"Sure. His voice was a little thick and he talked kind of funny. But he wasn't really drunk."

"That's all, Mr. Kaufman. Thank you."

They swore in the coroner's physician. He turned out to be the tall guy with the long thin nose, the one I'd thought looked like a faro dealer in a movie.

His name was Dr. William Haertel. His office was on Wabash and he lived on Division Street. Yes, he'd examined the body of the deceased.

What he said was technical. It boiled down to death from a blow on the head with a hard, blunt object. Apparently it had been struck by someone standing behind the deceased.

"At what time did you examine the body?"

"Two forty-five."

"How long would you say he had been dead at that time?"

"One to two hours. Probably closer to two."

A hand touched my shoulder, timidly, as I was leaving Heiden's. I looked around and said, "Hello, Bunny."

He looked more like a scared little rabbit than usual. We stepped to one side of the doorway and let the others go past us. He said, "Gee, Ed, I'm—You know what I mean. Is there anything I can do?"

I said, "Thanks, Bunny, but I guess not. Not a thing."

"How's Madge? How's she taking it?"

"Not too good. But—"

"Look, Ed, if there's anything at all I can do, call on me. I mean, I've got a little money in the bank—"

I said, "Thanks, Bunny, but we'll get by okay."

I was glad he'd asked me instead of Mom. Mom might have borrowed from him, and probably I'd have had to pay it back. If we didn't have it, we'd get by without it.

And Bunny didn't have money to lend out and not get back, because I knew what he was saving for. A little printing shop of his own was Bunny Wilson's dream, but it costs plenty to start one. It's a tough game to get started in, and it takes capital.

He said, "Should I drop around, Ed? To talk to you and Madge? Would she want me to?"

"Sure," I told him. "Mom likes you a lot. I guess you're about the only one of Pop's friends she really likes. Come around any time."

"I will, Ed. Maybe next week, my evening off. Wednesday. Your dad was a swell guy, Ed."

I liked Bunny, but I didn't want any more of that. I got away from him and went on home.

CHAPTER 5

OVER THE PHONE, Uncle Ambrose said, "Kid, how would you like to be a gun punk?"

I said, "Huh?"

"Hang on to your hat. You're going to be."

"I haven't got a gun and I'm not a punk."

He said, "You're half right. But you won't need a gun. All you're going to do is scare a guy half out of his wits."

"Sure it won't be me that's scared?"

"Go ahead and be scared. It'll stiffen you up and help the act. I'll give you some tips."

I asked, "Are you really serious?"

He said, "Yes," flatly, just like that, and I knew he was.

"When?" I asked him.

"We'll wait till day after tomorrow, after the funeral."

"Sure," I said.

After I'd hung up, I wondered what the hell I was letting myself in for. I wandered into the living room and turned on the radio. It was a gangster program and I turned it off again.

I thought, I'd make a hell of a gun punk.

Now that I'd had time to think it over, I had an idea what he meant. I was really a little scared.

It was Friday evening, after the inquest. Mom was down at the undertaker's, making final arrangements. I don't know where Gardie was. Probably a movie.

I went to the window and looked out. It was still raining.

In the morning it had stopped.

It was still damp and misty, and it was a hot muggy dampness. I put on my best clothes, of course, for the funeral, and they stuck to me like they were lined with glue.

I'd put my suit coat on, just to be all dressed, but I took it off and hung it up again until nearer time.

I thought, a gun punk. Maybe my uncle is a little nuts. All right, maybe I'm a little nuts too. I'll try it, whatever he wants.

I heard Mom getting up. I went out.

I stood looking at the outside of Heiden's.

After awhile, I went in. Mr. Heiden was in his office, in his shirt sleeves, working with some papers. He put down a cigar and said, "Hello. You're Ed Hunter, aren't you?"

"Yes," I said. "I wondered—I just wanted to know if there's anything I can do?"

He shook his head. "Everything's set, kid. Not a thing."

I said, "I didn't ask Mom. Have you got pallbearers and everything?"

"Fellows from the shop where he worked, yes. Here's the list."

He handed me a slip of paper and I read the names. The foreman at the shop, Jake Lancey, was at the top of the list, and three other linotype operators and two hand-men. I hadn't thought about the shop at all. It made me feel a little funny to find they were coming.

He said, "The funeral's at two. Everything's set. We're having an organist."

I nodded. "He liked organ music."

He said, "Sometimes, kid, members of the family would rather—well, take a last look and kind of say good-bye in private. Like now, and not file past the bier at the funeral. Maybe that's why you came in, kid?"

I guess it was. I nodded.

He took me into a room just off one of the halls, not the one where the inquest had been, but one the same size off the other side of the main corridor, and there was a coffin on a bier. It was a beautiful coffin. It was gray plush with chromium trimmings.

He lifted the part of the lid that uncovered the upper part of the body, and then he went out quietly, without saying anything.

I stood looking down at Pop.

After awhile, I put the lid down gently, and went out. I closed the door of the little room behind me. I got out of the place without seeing Mr. Heiden again, or anybody.

I started walking east, then south. I walked through the Loop and quite a way out on South State Street.

Then I slowed down and stopped, and started back again.

There were a lot of florists' shops in the Loop, and I remembered I hadn't done anything about flowers. I still had money from my pay check. I went in one and asked if they could send out some red roses right away for a funeral that would be in a few hours. They said they could.

After that, I stopped for a cup of coffee and then went home. I got there at about eleven.

The minute I opened the door I knew something was wrong.

I knew by the smell. The hot close air was full of whiskey. It smelled like West Madison Street on Saturday night.

My God, I thought. Three hours till the funeral.

I closed the door behind me, and for some reason I locked it. I went to the door of Mom's bedroom and I didn't knock. I opened it and looked in.

She was dressed, wearing the new black dress she must have bought yesterday. She was sitting on the edge of the bed, and there was a whiskey bottle in her hand. Her eyes looked dazed, stupid. They tried to focus on me.

She'd put her hair up, but it had come down again on one side. Her face muscles had gone lax and she looked old. She was drunk as hell.

She swayed a little back and forth.

I was across the room and had the whiskey bottle before she knew what was happening. But after I had it, she made a grab at it. She got up to come after it and nearly fell. I pushed her and she fell back on the bed. She started to curse me, and to get up again.

I got to the door, took out the key and put it in on the outside. I locked the door on the outside before she got hold of the knob.

I hoped Gardie was home; she *had* to be home to help me. She could handle Mom better than I could. I had to have help.

I ran into the kitchen first and held the whiskey bottle upside down over the sink and let it gurgle out. It seemed to me that the first thing I had to do was to get rid of the whiskey.

Mom's voice came from behind the locked door. She was cursing and crying and trying the knob. But she didn't yell and she didn't hammer; thank God she wasn't loud.

The doorknob quit rattling as I put down the empty bottle on the sink.

I started for Gardie's room and then there was another sound that stopped me cold.

It was a window going up. The window from Mom's bedroom into the airshaft.

She was going to jump.

I ran back and got hold of the key to unlock the door. It stuck a little, but the window was sticking too. That window had always stuck, had always been hard to open. I could hear her struggling with it. She was just sobbing now, not cursing or crying.

I got the door open and got there just as she was trying to go through. She'd got the window open only a little over a foot and it had stuck there, but she was trying to crawl through.

I yanked her back and she reached for my face to scratch me.

There was only one thing. I hit her on the chin, hard. I managed part way to catch her before she fell too hard. She was out cold.

I stood there a minute, trying to get my breath back, and trembling, cold clammy wet with sweat in that hot and stinking room.

Then I went for Gardie.

She'd slept through it. Somehow she'd slept through it. It was eleven o'clock and she was still sound asleep.

I shook her and she opened her eyes and then sat up. Her arms folded across her breasts in sudden modesty because she wasn't awake enough yet to be immodest and her eyes went wide.

I said, "Mom's drunk. Three hours to the funeral. Hurry up."

I handed her a wrapper or robe or whatever it was off the back of a chair, and hurried out. Her footsteps came right behind me.

I said, "In her bedroom. I'll get the water going." I went into the bathroom and turned on the cold water in the tub. I turned it on all the way; it would splash out for a while while the tub was empty, but to hell with that.

Back in the bedroom, Gardie had gone right to work. She was taking off Mom's shoes and stockings.

She asked, "How did she do it? Where were you?"

I said, "I was out from eight till just now. She must have got up about the time I left and gone right down and bought the bottle. She's had a full three-hour start."

I took Mom's shoulders and Gardie took her knees and we got her on the bed and started working her dress off over her head.

I got worried about something. I said, "She's got another slip she can wear, hasn't she?"

"Sure. Think we can get her around in time?"

"We got to. Leave her slip on then. The hell with it. Come on; we'll walk her to the bathroom."

She was a dead weight. We couldn't walk her. We had to half-carry half-drag her, finally, but we got her there.

The tub was full by then. Getting her into it was the hardest part. Gardie and I both got pretty wet, too. But we got her in.

I told Gardie, "Keep her head out. I'll start some coffee and make it thick as soup."

Gardie said, "Open a window in her room and let that smell out."

I said, "I did. I opened a window to air it out."

I turned on the fire under the kettle and put coffee in the pot ready to pour water through. I put in as much as it would hold, way up to the top.

I ran back to the bathroom. Gardie had tied a towel around Mom's hair and was splashing cold water in her face. She was waking up. She was moaning a little and trying to move her head to get away from the splashing water. She was shivering, and her arms and shoulders were covered with goose flesh from the cold water.

Gardie said, "She's coming around. But I don't know—My God, Eddie, three hours—"

"A little less," I said. "Listen, when she comes to, you can help her out of the tub and help her dry off. I'm going down to the drugstore. There's some stuff. I don't know what you call it."

I went in my room and quick put on a dry shirt and pair of pants. I'd have to wear my everyday suit to the funeral, but that couldn't be helped.

When I went by the bathroom the door was closed and I could hear Gardie's voice and Mom's. It was thick and fuzzy, but it wasn't hysterical and she wasn't cursing or anything. Maybe we can do it in time, I thought.

The coffee water was boiling. I poured it in the dripolator top and put a low bead of fire under the dripolator to keep it hot.

I went down to Klassen's drugstore. I figured I'd do better to level with him, because I knew him and I knew he wouldn't talk about it. So I told him enough of the truth.

"We got proprietary stuff," he said. "It's not so hot. I'll fix you something."

"Her breath, too," I said. "She'll have to be close to people at the funeral. You got to give me something for that."

We did it. We got her straightened out.

The funeral was beautiful.

I didn't mind it, really. It wasn't exactly Pop's funeral, to me. When I'd been alone with him, there in the little room, well, that was it, as far as I was concerned. I'd said good-bye to him, sort of, then.

This was just something you had to go through with, on account of other people and out of respect for Pop.

I sat on one side of Mom, and Gardie on the other. Uncle Ambrose sat next to me on the other side.

After the funeral, Jake, the foreman from the shop, came up to me. He said, "You're coming back, aren't you, Ed?"

"Sure," I said. "I'm coming back."

"Take as long as you want. Things are slow right now."

I said, "I've got something I want to do, Jake. Would a week or two weeks be all right?"

"As long as you want. Like I said, we're slack now. But don't change your mind about coming back. It won't be the same, working there, without your dad. But you're getting a good start at a good trade. We want you back."

"Sure," I said. "I'm coming back."

He said, "There's some stuff in your dad's locker. Shall we send it over to your place, or do you want to drop in and get it?"

"I'll drop in and get it," I said. "I want to pick up the check I've got coming for three days, too. Dad's got one too; Monday through Wednesday."

"I'll tell the office to have 'em both made out and ready for you, Ed," Jake said.

After the cemetery, after they'd thrown dirt on the coffin, Uncle Ambrose came home with us.

We sat around and there wasn't much to say. Uncle Ambrose suggested we play some cards, and he and Mom and I played for a little while. We played rummy.

When he left, I walked out in the hall with him. He said, "Take it easy this evening, kid. Rest up and get set for action. And look me up at the hotel tomorrow afternoon."

"Okay," I told him. "But isn't there anything I can do this evening?"

"Nope," he said. "I'm seeing Bassett, but no reason for you to go along. I'm going to put a bug in his ear about investigating who lives in those apartments with their back porches on the alley. He can do the spade work better than we can, and if there's a lead, we'll dig in there, too."

"Too? You mean, Kaufman?"

"Yeah. He was lying about something at the inquest. You saw that, didn't you?"

"I wasn't sure," I said.

"I was. That's where Bassett missed the boat. But we'll take care of it. Look me up about the middle of the afternoon. I'll wait in my room."

At about seven o'clock, Mom thought it might be a good idea if I took Gardie to a movie, down in the loop maybe.

I thought, why not?

Maybe Mom wanted to be alone. I studied her, without seeming to watch her, while Gardie was looking over the movie ads in the paper. Mom didn't look or act like she was getting ready to drink again.

She sure shouldn't want to, I thought, after this morning. That had been bad, but she'd snapped out of it beautifully. At the funeral she'd talked to people and everything and none of them could have guessed. I didn't think even Uncle Ambrose had guessed what had happened. Nobody but me and Gardie and Klassen, the druggist.

Her eyes had been red and her face puffy, but then they'd have been that way anyway from crying.

She really loved Pop, I thought.

Gardie wanted to go to a show that sounded like a mess of

mush to me, but there was a good swing orchestra on the stage, so I didn't argue.

I was right; the picture smelled. But the ork had a brass section that was out of the world. Way out. They had two trombones that knew what it was all about. One of them, the one that took solos, was as good as Teagarden, I thought. Maybe not on the fast stuff, but he had a tone that went down inside you.

I thought, I'd give a million bucks to do that, if I had a million bucks.

The finale was a jump number and Gardie's feet got restless. She wanted to go somewhere and dance, but I said nix. Going to a show was bad enough, the night of the day of the funeral.

When we got home, Mom wasn't there.

I read a magazine awhile, and then turned in.

I woke up in the middle of the night. There were voices. Mom's, pretty drunk. Another voice that sounded familiar but that I couldn't place.

It was none of my business but I was curious whose voice that was. I finally got out of bed and went to the door where I was closer. But the male voice quit talking and the door closed.

I hadn't heard a word of it, just the voices.

I heard Mom go into her room and close the door. From the way she walked she'd been drinking plenty, but she was under better control than this morning. She hadn't sounded hysterical or anything; the voices had been friendly.

I decided not to worry about the window.

Back in bed, I lay there for a long time thinking, trying to place that voice.

Then I got it. It was Bassett, the homicide dick, with the faded red hair and the faded eyes.

I wonder, I thought. Maybe he thinks she did it, and got her drunk to pump her. I didn't like that.

Maybe that wasn't the reason at all, and I don't know that I liked that any better. If Bassett was on the make, I mean. I remembered he'd said he had a sick wife.

I didn't like either one. And if he was combining business with pleasure, well—that made him more of a Grade A bastard than either one would alone. And I'd liked the guy. Even after he'd taken a bribe from Uncle Ambrose, I'd liked him.

I couldn't get to sleep for a while. I didn't like anything I thought of.

I woke up in the morning with a bad taste in my mouth.

There was still that muggy dampness in the air. I thought, am I going to wake up every morning at seven, whether I set that damn alarm or not?

It wasn't until I was up and getting dressed that it occurred to me Bassett might be okay after all. I mean, I could have been wrong on both counts. Mom could have gone out to make the rounds of Clark Street and he could have run into her accidentally and brought her home. For her own good, I mean.

I got dressed and I didn't know what to do.

While I was drinking coffee, Gardie came out into the kitchen.

"Hi, Eddie," she said, "Can't sleep. Might as well get up, huh?"

"Might as well," I agreed.

"Keep some coffee hot, will you?"

"Sure."

She went back to her room and dressed and then came and sat across the table from me. I poured her some coffee and she got a sweet roll from the breadbox.

"Eddie," she said.

"Yeah?"

"What time did Mom get home last night?"

"I don't know."

"You mean you didn't hear her come in at all?" She started to get up, like she was going to Mom's room to be sure she was there.

"She's home," I said. "I heard her come in. I just meant I didn't know what time it was. I didn't look at the clock."

"Pretty late, though?"

"I guess it was. I'd been asleep. She'll probably sleep till noon."

She nibbled at the roll thoughtfully. Always there'd be lipstick on the roll where she'd bitten it. I wondered why she bothered to put on lipstick before she ate breakfast.

"Eddie," she said. "I've got an idea."

"Yeah?"

"Mom drinks too much. If she keeps it up, well—"

There wasn't anything to say to that. I waited to see if there was any more coming. If not, it wasn't a particularly practical idea. I mean, there was nothing we could do about Mom's drinking.

Gardie looked at me with her eyes wide. "Eddie, there was a pint in her dresser drawer a couple of days ago. I took it and hid it and she never missed it. She must've forgot about it."

"Pour it out," I said.

"She'll buy more, Eddie. It costs a dollar forty-nine. And she'll just buy more."

"Then she'll buy more," I said. "So what?"

"Eddie, I'm going to *drink* it."

"You're crazy. My God, you're fourteen, and you—"

"I'm fifteen, Eddie. Next month. That's fifteen. And I have

had drinks, on dates. I never got drunk, but—Listen, Eddie, don't you see?"

"Not with a telescope," I said. "You're crazy."

"Eddie, Pop drank too much, too."

"Leave Pop out of it," I told her. "That's over with. Anyway, what the hell's that got to do with your drinking? You mean you think you've got to carry on the family tradition, or something?"

"Don't be dumb, Eddie. What do you think would have stopped Pop drinking?"

I was getting a little mad at her for harping on that. Pop was out of this. Pop was six feet underground.

She said, "I'll tell you what might have stopped Pop, Eddie. If he'd seen you starting the same way. You were always goody-goody. He knew you'd never go haywire, the way he did. I mean, suppose you'd started coming home drunk, too, running with a wild gang— He might have stopped drinking, so you would. He loved you, Eddie. If he thought what he was doing was making you into a—"

"Can it," I said. "Damn it, Pop's dead and why bring up screwy ideas now?"

"Mom isn't dead. Maybe you don't think much of her, but she's my mother, Eddie."

I'd been dumb, sure. It actually took me that long to see what she was driving at.

I just sat there looking at her. There was a chance, maybe an off chance, that it would work. That if Gardie started going haywire that way, it would sort of wake Mom up. She'd lost Pop, but she still had Gardie and she sure as hell wouldn't want to see Gardie getting stinking drunk at fifteen.

Then I thought, the hell with it. That's no way of doing it.

But I had to give Gardie credit for thinking of it. She's been thinking about it, I could see.

"Nuts," I said. "You can't do it."

"The hell I can't, Eddie. I'm going to."

"You're not." But I thought, I can't stop her. She's thought this over and she's going to do it. I could maybe stop her now, but I can't stay around and watch her all the time.

"Now's a good time, Eddie," she said. "When she wakes up at noon with a hangover, she'll find me tight. You think she's going to like that?"

"She'll beat the hell out of you."

"How can she, when she does it herself? She wouldn't beat me anyway. She never did."

Maybe, I thought, it would be better if she had.

I said, "I don't want any part of it." I thought maybe I could get her mad. I said, "It's a gag anyway. You just want to get drunk to see what it's like."

She pushed her chair back. "I'm going to get the bottle. You can make like a goody-goody and take it away and break it. If you do, I'll go down on Clark Street and get drunk. I look older'n I am, and there are plenty of places where they'll buy a girl all the drinks she wants. And they won't be B-drinks."

Her heels clicked toward her room.

Get the hell out of this, Eddie, I told myself. You don't want any part of it. And she can and will get drunk on Clark Street if you stick your oar in. And probably end up at a whorehouse in Cicero. And like it.

I got up but I didn't go out.

I was on the spot. I couldn't stop her drinking, but I'd have to stick around to keep her out of trouble. When she hit a certain stage, she'd sure as hell want to go out. I couldn't let her do that.

I was stuck with it.

She came back with the bottle. It had already been opened. She poured herself a drink.

She asked, "Have one, Eddie?"

I said, "I thought this was business."

"You could be sociable."

"I'm not," I told her.

She laughed and drank it down. She grabbed for a glass of water for a chaser, but she didn't choke or anything.

She poured another and then sat down.

She grinned at me. "Sure you don't want to come along?"

I said, "Nuts."

She laughed and drank the other one. She went into the living room and turned on the radio, monkeying with the dials until she got some music. It was good music for that time in the morning.

She said, "Come on, Eddie. Dance with me. It works faster if you dance."

"I don't want to dance."

"Goody-goody."

"Nuts," I said.

I saw it coming.

She took a few fancy pirouettes by herself, to the music, and then came back and sat down. She poured the third one.

"Not so fast," I said. "You can kill yourself guzzling that stuff fast when you're not used to it."

"I've drunk before. Not much, but some." She got another glass and poured some whiskey in it. "Come on, Eddie, have just one. Please. It ain't nice to have to drink alone."

"All right," I said. "Just one. I mean it."

She'd picked up her glass and said, "Happy days," and I had to pick up mine and touch the rims. I took just a sip, but she downed hers.

She went back to the radio. She called, "Come on in here, Eddie. Bring the glasses and the bottle."

I went in and sat down. She sat down on the arm of my chair.

"Pour me another, Eddie. This is fun."

"Yeah," I said. I took a sip of my drink while she downed her fourth. She choked a little on that one.

"Eddie," she said, "please dance with me."

The music was good.

I said, "Cut it out, Gardie. Cut it out."

She got up and started to dance by herself to the music, swinging and dipping and swaying around the room.

She said, "Some day I'm going on the stage, Eddie. What do you think? How'm I doin'?"

"You dance swell," I told her.

"Bet I could strip-tease. Like Gypsy Rose. Watch." She reached behind her, as she danced, for the fastenings of her dress.

I said, "Don't be a dope, Gardie. I'm your brother, remember?"

"You're not my brother. Anyway, what's that got to do with how I dance? How—"

She was having trouble with the catch. She danced near me. I reached out and grabbed her hand. I said, "Goddam it, Gardie, cut that out."

She laughed and leaned back against me. The pull on her wrist had brought her into my lap.

She said, "Kiss me, Eddie." Her lips were bright red, her

body hot against mine. And then her lips were pressing against mine, without my doing anything about it.

I managed to stand up. I said, "Gardie, goddam it, stop. You're only a kid. We *can't.*"

She pulled away and laughed a little. "All right, Eddie. All right. Let's have another drink, huh?"

I poured us two drinks. I handed her one. I said, "Here's to Mom, Gardie."

She said, "Okay, Eddie. Anything you say."

This time it was I that choked on it, and she laughed at me.

She took a few more dance steps. She said, "Pour me another, Eddie. Be back in a minute."

She weaved a little on the way through the door.

I poured two drinks, and then went over to the radio and fiddled with it. I switched programs and then switched back again. There wasn't anything else on but plays.

I didn't hear her come back till she said, "Eddie," and then I looked around.

The reason I hadn't heard her come back was that she was barefoot. She was stark naked.

She said, "Am I only a kid, Eddie?" She laughed a little. "Am I only a kid, huh?"

I quit fiddling with the radio. I shut it off.

I said, "You ain't a kid, Gardie. So let's kill the bottle first. Okay? Here's your drink."

I handed it to her and then I went out in the kitchen for water for chasers, and pretended I drank mine while I was out there, and came back with two more.

She said, "I feel—woozy."

"Here," I said. "This is good for it. Bottoms up, Gardie."

I drank that one with her. There was only about one shot left in the bottle; we must have been pouring really stiff ones.

She started to take a dance step toward me, and stumbled. I had to catch her, my arms around her and my hands on her.

I helped her to the sofa. I started back for the bottle. She said, "S'down, Eddie. S'dow. C'm—"

"Sure," I said, "sure. One more drink apiece left. Let's kill it, huh?"

Most of it went on the outside of her, but some got down. She giggled when I wiped off the whiskey with my handkerchief.

"Feel woozy, E'ie. Woozy—"

"Close your eyes a minute," I said. "You'll be all right."

A minute was enough. She was all right.

I picked her up and carried her into her room. I found the bottoms of her pajamas and got them on her, and then I closed the door.

I rinsed out the glasses and put the bottle out of sight in the step-on garbage can.

Then I got the hell out.

CHAPTER 6

IT WAS ABOUT TWO O'CLOCK when I took the elevator at the Wacker to the twelfth floor, found Uncle Ambrose's room and knocked.

He looked at me closely as he let me in. He asked, "What's wrong, Ed? What you been doing?"

"Nothing," I said. "I've just been walking. Took a long walk."

"Nothing wrong? Where'd you go?"

"Nowhere," I said. "I just walked."

"Exercise?"

"Cut it out," I said. "Let me alone."

"Sure, kid. I didn't mean to butt in. Sit down and relax."

"I thought we were going out to do something."

"Sure, we are. But there's no rush." He took out a crumpled pack of cigarettes. "Have one?"

"Sure."

We lighted up.

He stared at me through smoke. He said, "You're kind of fed up with everything, aren't you, kid? I don't know exactly what set it off, but I might make a guess. One of your women threw a wingding, or maybe both of them. Was it you sobered up Madge for the funeral?"

I said, "You don't have to wear glasses, do you?"

He said, "Kid, Madge and Gardie are what they are. There's nothing you can do about it."

"It's not all Mom's fault," I said. "I guess she just can't help the way she is."

"It's never all anybody's fault, kid. You'll learn that. That goes for Wally. It goes for you. It isn't your fault you're what you are."

"What am I?"

"You're bitter. Black bitter. Not just because of Wally, either. I think it was before that. Kid, go over and take a look out of that window a minute."

His room was on the south side of the hotel. I went over and looked out. It was still foggy, gray. But you could see south to the squat, monstrous Merchandise Mart Building, and between the Wacker and it the ugly west near-north side. Mostly ugly old brick buildings hiding ugly lives.

"It's a hell of a view," I told him.

"That's what I meant, kid. When you look out of a window, when you look at anything, you know what you're seeing? Yourself. A thing can look beautiful or romantic or inspiring only if the beauty or romance or inspiration is inside you. What you see is inside your head."

I said, "You talk like a poet, not a carney."

He chuckled. "I read a book once," he said. "Look, kid, don't try to label things. Words fool you. You call a guy a printer or a lush or a pansy or a truck driver and you think you've pasted a label on him. People are complicated; you *can't* label 'em with a word."

I was still standing at the window, but I'd turned around to face him. He got up off the bed and came over by me. He turned me around to look out the window again and stood there by me with his hand on my shoulder.

He said, "Look down there, kid. I want to show you another way of looking at it. The way that'll do you some good right now."

We stood there looking down out of the open window into the steaming streets.

He said, "Yeah, I read a book once. You've read this too, but maybe you never really looked at things the way they are, even if you know. That looks like something down there, doesn't it? Solid stuff, each chunk of it separate from the next one and air in between them.

"It isn't. It's just a mess of atoms whirling around and the atoms are just made up of electric charges, electrons, whirling around too, and there's space between them like there's space between the stars. It's a big mess of almost nothing, that's all. And there's no sharp line where the air stops and a building begins; you just think there is. The atoms get a little less far apart.

"And besides whirling, they vibrate back and forth, too. You think you hear noise, but it's just those awful-far-apart atoms wiggling a little faster.

"Look, there's a guy walking down Clark Street. Well, he isn't anything, either. He's just a part of the dance of the atoms, and he blends in with the sidewalk below him and the air around him."

He went back and sat down on the bed. He said, "Keep looking, kid. Get the picture. What you think you see is just bally, a front with the gimmicks all hidden if there are any gimmicks.

"A continuous mess of almost nothing, that's what's really

there. Space between molecules. Enough solid, actual matter, if any, to make a chunk about the size of a—a soccer ball."

He chuckled. "Kid," he said. "You going to let a soccer ball kick you around?"

I kept standing there looking for another minute or so. When I turned around he was laughing at me, and I found myself grinning.

"Okay," I said. "Shall we go down and kick Clark Street around for a change?"

"Chicago Avenue. A spot near Orleans. We're going to scare hell out of a guy named Kaufman."

I said, "He's run bar in a tough neighborhood for a lot of years. What kind of threat would scare a guy like that?"

"None. We're not going to threaten a damn thing. That's what'll scare him stiff. It's the one thing that will."

"I don't get it," I told him. "Maybe I'm dumb, but I don't get it?"

"Come on," he said.

"What are we going to do?"

"Nothing. Not a damn thing. Just sit in his place."

I still didn't get it, but I could wait. We went down in the elevator.

As we crossed the lobby, he asked, "Can you use a new suit, Ed?"

"Sure, but I'd better not buy one now. I'm losing time off work."

"It's on me. You need a dark-blue, pin-stripe cut so it'll make you look older. You need the right kind of a hat. It's part of the job, kid, so don't squawk. You got to look like a gun punk."

"Okay," I said. "But I'll owe you for it. Someday I'll pay you."

We got the suit, and it cost forty bucks. That was nearly

twice what I'd paid for my last one. Uncle Ambrose was particular about the style; we looked at quite a few before he found the one he wanted.

He told me, "That isn't too good a suit; it won't last very long. But while it's brand new, before it gets dry-cleaned, it looks like an expensive suit. Come on, we get a hat."

We got a hat, a dilly of a snap-brim. He wanted to buy me shoes, but I talked him into settling for a shine; the ones I had were nearly new and looked good once they were shined. We got a rayon shirt that looked like silk, and a snazzy tie.

Back at the hotel, I changed into the new stuff and took a gander at myself in the mirror on the bathroom door.

Uncle Ambrose said, "Wipe off that grin, you dope. It makes you look sweet sixteen."

I straightened out my face. "How's the hat look?"

"Swell. Where'd you get it?"

"Huh? Herzfeld's."

"Try again and think harder. You got it in Lake Geneva the last time I took you up there. We were a little hot then, or we thought we were. We holed out a week till Blane wired us the heat was off. Remember the hat-check girl at the roadhouse?"

"The little brunette?"

He nodded. "Coming back to you now, huh? Sure, she bought you that hat after yours blew out of the car that night. Why shouldn't she? You spent about three hundred bucks on her that week. Hell, you wanted to bring her back to Chi with you."

I said, "I still think I should have. Why didn't I?"

"I told you not to, see? And I'm the boss; get that through your head and keep it there. Kid, you'd have fried two years ago if I didn't look out for you. I keep you from getting too big for your pants. Sure, I—Goddam it, get that grin off your mug."

"Yeah, Chief. What would I have fried for?"

"The Burton Bank job for one thing. You're always too quick on the trigger. When that teller reached for the button, you could've shot his arm as easy as killing him; you were only a few feet away."

I said, "The bastard shouldn't reached."

"And the time I had you take care of Swann when he got out of line. What'd you do? Just plug him? No, you had to get fancy about it. Remember that?"

"He got funny. He asked for it."

He looked at me and shook his head. His voice changed. He said, "It ain't bad, Ed. But you're too relaxed. I want you stiff, jumpy. You've got a heater in that shoulder holster, and it's loaded. The weight of it there won't let you forget it. Keep that heater on your mind, every minute."

"Sure," I said.

"And your eyes. Ever watched a guy's eyes after he's had about two reefers? And before he's smoked more than that?"

I nodded slowly.

He said, "Then you know what I mean. He's the king of the universe, and he's hot as a G string. But he's like a coiled spring, tied down by a thin thread. He can sit still with a kind of unholy calm, and still make you afraid to touch him with a ten-foot pole."

"I think I got it," I told him.

"Keep your eyes like that. When you look at a guy, you don't glare at him like you want to kill him. That's ham stuff. You just look *through* him like he wasn't there, like you don't give a damn whether you shoot him or not. Look at him like he was a telegraph pole."

"How about tone of voice?" I asked.

"Nuts to tone of voice. Keep your trap shut. Don't even talk to me, unless I ask you something. I'll do the talking and it won't be much."

He looked at his watch and got up off the bed. He said, "It's five o'clock, shank of the morning for this neighborhood. Let's go."

"Will this take all evening?"

"Maybe longer."

I said, "I want to use your phone, then. It's kind of private. Will you go on down and wait for me in the lobby?"

He said, "Sure, kid," and went on out.

I called home. If Mom answered I'd have hung up. I didn't want to talk to Mom before I found out what Gardie had told her.

But it was Gardie's voice.

I said, "This is Ed, Gardie. Is Mom around, or can you talk?"

"She went to the store. Oh, Eddie—did I—make an awful fool of myself?"

It was going to be all right.

I said, "Kind of, but let's forget it. You got tight, that's all. But no more, savvy? You try that again and I'll take a hairbrush to you."

She giggled a little. Or it might have been a giggle.

I said, "Does Mom know you drank that whiskey?"

"No, Eddie. I woke up first. I felt like hell—I still don't feel so good. But I managed not to show it—Mom woke up feeling awful herself, so she didn't notice. I told her I had a headache."

"What happened to that bright idea about teaching her a lesson?"

"I forgot, Eddie, I clean forgot. I felt so lousy all I thought about was keeping out of Mom's way. I just couldn't have stood her bawling me out, or crying, or whatever she'd've done."

"Okay," I said. "So forget the idea permanently. *Both* ideas, if you know what I mean. You remember what you did when you were drunk?"

"N-not exactly, Eddie. What *did* I do?"

"Don't kid me," I said. "You remember all right."

Unmistakably, this time, it was a giggle.

I gave up. I said, "Listen, tell Mom I won't be home till late, probably, but not to worry. I'll be with Uncle Am. I might even stay with him over night. So long."

I hung up before she could ask any questions.

Going down in the elevator, I tried to get my mind back in the groove. Uncle Ambrose had been right in picking the clothes and the hat. I looked twenty-two or twenty-three in the elevator mirror, and I looked like I'd been around.

I stiffened up, and made my eyes hard.

My uncle nodded approvingly as I walked across the lobby toward him.

He said, "You'll do, kid. Damn if I'm not a little leary of you myself."

We walked north to Chicago Avenue and turned west. We went past the police station. I kept my eyes straight in front.

As we crossed diagonally over at Chicago and Orleans, heading for the Topaz beer sign, my uncle said, "All I want you to do is this, Ed. Don't talk. Watch Kaufman. Follow my leads."

"Sure," I said.

We went into the tavern. Kaufman was drawing beers for

two men at the bar. There was a man and woman sitting in a booth at the side; they looked married. The two men at the bar looked a little drunk in a sleepy sort of way, like they'd been drinking beer all afternoon. They were together, but weren't talking.

Uncle Ambrose headed for a table at the back, sitting so he could face the bar. I pulled a chair to one side of the table, so I could face the same way.

I watched Kaufman.

He wasn't, I thought, particularly pleasant to look at. He was short and heavy-set, with long arms that looked powerful. He looked about forty or forty-five. He wore a clean white shirt with the sleeves rolled to the elbows, and his arms were hairy as a monkey's. His hair was slicked back and glossy, but he needed a shave. He still wore the thick-lensed glasses.

He rang up twenty cents on the register for the two beers he'd just drawn and then came around the end of the bar and approached our table.

I kept my eyes on him, studying him, weighing him.

He looked tough, like a guy able to handle himself in trouble. But then most bartenders in this part of town look like that; or they wouldn't be bartenders here.

He said, "What's it, gents?"

His eyes happened to fall on mine, and I locked them there. I remembered orders. I didn't move a muscle, not even a muscle of my face. But I thought, "You son of a bitch, I'd just as soon kill you as not."

Uncle Ambrose was saying, "White soda. Two glasses of plain white soda."

His eyes slid off mine and looked at my uncle. He looked

doubtful, not knowing whether to take it for a joke and laugh, or not.

Uncle Ambrose didn't laugh. He said, "Two glasses of white soda."

He dropped a bill on the table.

Kaufman managed somehow to seem to shrug his shoulders without really doing it. He took the bill and went behind the bar. He came back with the two glasses and change.

"Anything for a wash?" he wanted to know.

Uncle Ambrose deadpanned him. He said, "When we want something else, we'll let you know."

Kaufman went back of the bar again.

We sat there and didn't do anything and didn't talk. Once in a long while Uncle Ambrose took a sip of his white soda.

The two men at the bar went out and another group, three this time, came in. We didn't pay any attention to them. We watched Kaufman; I don't mean we didn't take our eyes off him for a second, but in general we just sat there watching him.

You could see, after awhile, that it began to puzzle him, and that he didn't like it a damn bit.

Two more men came in, and the couple sitting in the booth left.

At seven o'clock a bartender came on duty. A tall, skinny man who smiled a lot and showed a lot of gold teeth when he did. When he went behind the bar, Kaufman came over to our table.

"Two more white sodas," my uncle said.

Kaufman looked at him a moment, then he picked up the change my uncle put on the table and went behind the bar to refill our glasses. He came back and put them down without a word. Then he took off his apron, hung it on a hook and went out the back door of the tavern.

"Think he's going for the cops?"

My uncle shook his head. "He isn't that worried yet. He's going out to eat. Think that's a good idea?"

"Good Lord," I said. I just remembered that this was another day I'd practically gone without eating. Now that I thought of it, I was hungry enough to eat a cow.

We waited a few minutes longer and then went out the front way. We walked over to Clark Street and ate at the little chili joint a block south of Chicago. They make the best chili there of any place in town.

We took our time about eating. While we were drinking coffee, I asked, "We going back there tonight?"

"Sure. We'll get back by nine and stay till about twelve. He'll be getting jittery by then."

"Then what?"

"We help him jitter."

"Look," I said. "What if he does call copper? Yeah, there's nothing illegal about sitting a few hours over white soda, but if the cops get called, they'll want to ask questions."

"The cops are squared. Bassett's talked to the looie who'd get the call at the Chicago station. He'll tip off whatever coppers he sends in answer to the call, if he sends any."

I said, "Oh." I began to see about the hundred bucks. This was the first dividend, unless you counted that Bassett had said he'd canvass the buildings that had back porches on the alley. Maybe he'd have done that anyway, but squaring something like this was definitely in the line of extra service.

After we ate, we went to a quiet little place off Clark Street on Ontario and had a beer apiece and a lot of conversation.

We talked about Pop mostly.

"He was a funny kid, Ed," Uncle Ambrose told me. "He was two years younger than me, you know. He was wild as a colt. Well, I had itchy feet, too. I still have; that's why I'm a carney. You like to travel, Ed?"

"I think I would," I said. "I never had much chance up to now."

"Up to now? Hell, you're just a pup. But about Wally. He ran away from home when he was sixteen. That was the year our dad got a stroke and died suddenly; our mother had died three years before.

"I knew Wally'd write sooner or later, so I stuck around St. Paul until I got a letter from him, addressed to both me and Dad. He was in Petaluma, California. He owned a little newspaper there; he'd won it in a poker game."

"He never told me about that," I said.

My uncle chuckled. "He didn't have it long. He was gone by the time my wire went out in answer to his letter. I'd told him I was coming, but when I got there he was wanted by the police. Oh, nothing too serious; just a hell of a swell criminal libel action. He was too honest to run a newspaper. He'd come out with the flat, unvarnished truth about one of Petaluma's leading citizens. Probably just for the hell of it; anyway, that's what he told me later and I believed him."

He grinned at me. "It was a swell excuse for me to go on the road awhile, to look for him. I knew he'd head out of California, because the libel business wasn't something they were going to extradite him for, but he'd get out of the state. I picked up his trail in Phoenix, and I was just behind him several places before I ran into him in a gambling joint across the border from El

Paso, in Juarez. Juarez was a wild and woolly spot in those days, kid. You should have seen it."

"I suppose he lost whatever he'd pulled out of the newspaper."

"Huh? Oh, he'd lost that long before. He was working at the gambling joint. Dealing blackjack. He was fed up with Juarez by the time I got there, so he quit the dealing. He was picking up Mex and wanted me to head with him for Veracruz.

"Kid, that was a trip. Veracruz is a good twelve or thirteen hundred miles from Juarez and it took us four months to make it. We left Juarez with a stake of, I think, eighty-five bucks between us. But that changed into about four hundred bucks Mex, and while it wasn't much on the border, it made you rich when you got a hundred or so miles in, if you talked the lingo and didn't get yourself into the sucker joints.

"We were rich for half of that four months, nigger rich. Then in Monterrey we ran into some guys that were smarter than we were. We should have headed back for the border then, for Laredo, but we'd decided on Veracruz and we kept going. We got there on foot, in Mex clothes, what there was of them, and we hadn't had a peso between us in three weeks. We'd damn near forgotten how to talk English; we jabbered spik even to each other, to get better at it.

"We got jobs in Veracruz and straightened out. That's where your dad picked up linotype, Ed. A Spanish-language paper run by a German who had a Swedish wife and who'd been born in Burma. He needed a man who was fluent in both English and Spanish—he didn't speak much English himself—so he taught Wally how to run his linotype and the flat-bed press he printed the paper on."

I said, "I'll be damned."

"What now?"

I laughed a little. I said, "I took Latin in high school. Pop suggested Spanish when I started taking a language and said he could help me with it. I thought he remembered a little from having taken it in school himself. I never realized he could *talk* it."

Uncle Ambrose looked at me very seriously, as though he were thinking, and didn't say anything for a while.

I asked after awhile, "Where did you go from Veracruz?"

"I went to Panama; he stayed in Veracruz for a while. There was something about Veracruz that he liked."

"Did he stay there long?"

"No," said my uncle shortly. He glanced up at the clock. "Come on, kid, we better get back to Kaufman's."

I looked at the clock too. I said, "We got time. You said we'd get back at nine. If there was something about Veracruz he liked, and he had a job, why didn't he stay there long?"

Uncle Ambrose looked at me for a moment and then his eyes twinkled a little. He said, "I don't suppose Wally would mind your knowing now."

"All right, give."

"He had a duel, and he won. The thing he liked about Veracruz was the wife of the German who ran the newspaper. The German challenged him to a duel, with Mausers, and he couldn't get out of it. He won the duel all right; hit the German in the shoulder and put him in the hospital. But Wally had to get out of there quick. And privately, in the cargo hold of a tramp steamer. I learned from him later what happened. They caught him four days out and he had to work his passage swabbing decks when he was so seasick he couldn't stand up. Wally never could stand the sea. But he couldn't jump ship till they docked for the first time. That was in Lisbon."

"You're kidding me," I said.

"Nope. Fact, Ed. He was in Spain awhile. Had a screwy idea he wanted to learn to be a matador, but he couldn't get an in; you got to start at that trade really young and have some pull even then. Besides, the picador part disgusted him."

"What's a picador?" I asked.

"The lancemen, on horseback. Horses get gored almost every fight. They fill 'em with sawdust and sew 'em up so they can go back in. They won't live anyhow, once they're deeply gored, and so—Hell, skip it; I always hated that part of bull-fighting myself. Last card I saw though, down in Juarez a few years ago, they pad the horses and that part's okay. A clean kill of the bull with the sword; that's all right. It's better than they do in the stockyards here, for that matter. They use a—"

"Let's stick to Pop," I suggested. "He was in Spain."

"Yeah. Well, he came back. We finally got in touch with one another through a friend back in St. Paul we both happened to write to. I was with a detective agency then—Wheeler's, out in L.A.—and Wally was in vaudeville. He used to be pretty good at juggling—oh, not a top act, even as jugglers go, but he was good with the Indian clubs. Good enough for a spot with a fair troupe. He ever juggle any lately?"

"No," I said. "No, he didn't."

"You got to keep up on something like that, or you lose it. But he was always good at anything with his hands. He used to be a swift on the linotype. Was he still?"

"Average speed is all," I said. I thought of something. "Maybe it was because he had arthritis in his hands and arms for a while, quite a few years ago. He couldn't work at all for a few months, and maybe that slowed him down from then on. That was while we were in Gary, just before we moved from Gary to Chicago."

Uncle Ambrose said, "He never told me that."

I asked, "Did you and he ever get together again, outside of visits, I mean?"

"Oh, sure. I was in dutch with the shamus outfit already, so I quit and Wally and I traveled together with a medicine show. He did juggling and stuff, in blackface."

"Can you juggle?"

"Me, no? Wally was the one who could use his hands. Me, I make with the mouth. I did spieling, and put on a vent act."

I must have looked pretty blank.

He grinned at me. "Ventriloquism, to you mooches. Come on, kid, we really got to move on. If you want the story of my life and Wally's, you can't have it in one sitting when we got a spot of work ahead. It's almost nine now."

I walked to Kaufman's in a sort of a daze.

I'd never known that Pop had been anything but a linotype operator. I just couldn't think of him as a wild kid, bumming across Mexico, having a duel, wanting to be a bull-fighter in Spain, juggling with a medicine show, being part of a vaudeville troupe.

All that, I thought, and he died in an alley, drunk.

CHAPTER 7

KAUFMAN'S PLACE WAS BUSIER. There were half a dozen men and two women at the bar, couples in two of the booths, and a pinochle game at a back table. The juke box was blaring.

Our table, though, was empty. We sat just as we had before. Kaufman was busy at the bar; he didn't see us come in or sit down.

He saw us, and met our eyes watching him, a minute or so later. He was pouring whiskey into a jigger glass in front of a man at the bar and the whiskey came up over the rim of the glass and made a little puddle on the varnished wood.

He rang up the sale, then came around the end of the bar and stood in front of us, hands on his hips and looking belligerent and undecided at the same time.

He pitched his voice low. "What do you guys want?"

Uncle Ambrose took it deadpan. There wasn't a trace of humor in his face or in his voice. He said, "Two white sodas."

Kaufman took his hands off his hips and wiped them slowly on his apron. His eyes went from my uncle's face to mine and I gave him the flat, level stare.

He didn't meet it long. He looked back at Uncle Ambrose.

He pulled out a chair and sat down. He said, "I don't want any trouble here."

Uncle Ambrose said, "We don't like trouble either. We don't want any. We wouldn't make any."

"You want *something*. Wouldn't it be a lot easier if you levelled?"

"About what?" my uncle asked.

The tavern-owner's lips went together tight for a second. He looked like he was going to get mad.

Then his voice was calmer than before. He said, "I've placed you. You were at the inquest on that guy got slugged in an alley."

My uncle asked, "What guy?"

Kaufman took in a deep breath and let it out slowly. He said, "Yeah, I'm sure. You were in the back row, trying to keep outa sight. You a friend of this Hunter guy, or what?"

"What Hunter guy?"

Kaufman looked like he was going to get mad again, then he pulled in his horns.

He said, "Lemme save you trouble. Whatever you want, it ain't here. I ain't got it. I levelled with the coppers and at the inquest. I don't know a damn thing about it I didn't tell 'em. And you heard it; you was there."

My uncle didn't say anything. He took out a pack of cigarettes and handed it toward me. I took one, and he held it out to Kaufman. Kaufman ignored it.

Kaufman said, "It's all on the level. So what you coming in here for? What the hell do you want?"

Uncle Ambrose didn't bat an eyelash. He said, "White soda. Two glasses."

Kaufman stood up so suddenly that the chair he'd been sitting on went over backwards. Redness was spreading upward from his neck. He turned around and picked up the chair, pushing it back under the table carefully, as though its exact position there was a matter of importance.

He went back of the bar without saying another word.

A few minutes later the bartender, the tall skinny guy, brought our white sodas. He grinned cheerfully and my uncle grinned back. The little wrinkles of hell-with-it laughter were back around the corners of his eyes and he didn't look deadly at all.

Kaufman wasn't looking our way; he was busy at the other end of the bar.

"No Mickey?" Uncle Ambrose asked him.

"No Mickey," said the bartender. "You couldn't make a Mickey with plain white soda so it wouldn't taste."

"That's what I figured," said my uncle. He handed the slim guy a dollar bill. "Keep the change, Slim, for the baby's bank."

"Sure, thanks. Say, the kid was nuts about you, Am. Wants to know when you'll be out again."

"Soon, Slim. Better run along before his nibs sees us talking."

The bartender went back to the pinochle table to take their order.

I asked, "When did all this happen?"

"Last night. His evening off. Got his name and address from Bassett and went calling. He's on our side now."

"Another hundred bucks?"

My uncle shook his head. "There are guys you can buy, kid, and guys you can't. I managed to put a little silver in his kid's bank."

"Then that wasn't a gag about the kid's bank—I mean, about keeping the change out of the buck?"

"Hell, no. That's exactly where that change will go."

"I'll be damned," I said.

Kaufman was coming to the near end of the bar again, and I shut up and went back to watching him. He didn't look our way again.

We stayed there until a little after midnight. Then we got up and walked out.

When I got home, Mom and Gardie were asleep. There was a note from Mom asking me to wake her whenever I got up, because she wanted to start looking for a job.

I was tired, but I had trouble getting to sleep. I kept thinking about what I'd learned about Pop.

When he was my age, I thought, he'd owned and run a newspaper. He'd had a duel and shot a man. He'd had an affair with a married woman. He'd traveled across most of Mexico afoot and spoke Spanish like a native. He'd crossed the Atlantic and lived in Spain. He'd dealt blackjack in a border town.

When he was my age, I thought, he'd been in vaudeville and was traveling with a medicine show.

I couldn't picture Pop in blackface. I couldn't picture any of the rest of it, either. I wondered what he'd looked like then.

But when I slept, finally, I didn't dream about Pop. I dreamed about me, and I was a matador in a bull ring in Spain. I had black grease paint on my face and a rapier in my hand. And, mixed up like dreams are mixed up, the bull was a real bull—a huge black bull—and yet he wasn't. Somehow, he was a tavern owner named Kaufman.

He came running at me and his horns were a yard long, with points as sharp as needles, and they gleamed in the sunlight, and I was scared, scared as hell . . ..

We went back to the tavern at three o'clock the next afternoon. Uncle Ambrose had learned that was about the time Kaufman came on. Slim went off duty then, and came back later in the evening when things got busy enough to need two men.

Kaufman was just tying on his apron, and Slim must have just left, when we walked into the place.

He just glanced at us casually, as though he expected us.

There wasn't anyone else there; just Kaufman and us. But there was something in the atmosphere, something besides the smell of beer and whiskey.

There's going to be trouble, I thought.

I was scared, as scared as I'd been in my dream last night. I thought of it then, the dream.

We sat down at the table. The same table.

Kaufman came back. He said, "I don't want trouble. Why don't you guys move along?"

My uncle said, "We like it here."

"Okay," Kaufman said. He went back of the bar and came back with two glasses of white soda. My uncle gave him twenty cents.

He went back of the bar and started polishing glasses. He didn't look toward us. Once he dropped a glass and broke it.

A little later the door opened and two men came in.

They were big guys and they looked tough. One of them was an ex-pug; you could tell by his ears. He had a bullet head and shoulders like an ape. He had little pig eyes.

The other one looked small, standing by the big guy. But only by contrast; a second look told you he was five-eleven or so, and would go one-eighty stripped. He had a face like a horse.

They stopped just inside the door and looked the place over.

Their eyes took in all the booths and saw they were empty. They looked everywhere except at us. My uncle moved in his chair, shifted his feet.

Then they went over to the bar.

Kaufman put two shot glasses in front of them and filled the glasses without their having said a word.

That was the give-away, if there'd be any need for one.

There was a growing cold feeling in the pit of my stomach. I wondered if my legs would wobble if I stood up.

I glanced out of the corner of my eye at Uncle Ambrose. His face was perfectly still, his lips weren't moving, but he was talking, just loud enough that I could hear him. It surprised me for a moment that his mouth didn't move, until I remembered the vent business.

He said, "Kid, I can handle this better alone. You go back to the can. There's a window; get out of it and scram. Right now; soon as they've had a drink, they'll make a play."

He was lying, I knew. Unless he was heeled there wasn't a way on earth he could handle this. And he wasn't heeled, any more than I was.

I thought, I'm the one that's supposed to be heeled. I'm the gun punk. I've got a new suit that looks like a hundred bucks and a new snap-brim hat. And I've got an imaginary thirty-eight automatic, with the safety catch off. It's in a shoulder holster on my left shoulder.

I stood up, and my legs weren't rubber.

I walked around back of Uncle Ambrose's chair and started for the door of the men's room, but I didn't go there. I stopped short right at the end of the bar, and stood there where I could watch up the bar, front and back.

I'd brought up my right hand and let it rest with the fingers just inside my coat, touching the butt of the thirty-eight automatic that wasn't there.

I didn't say anything; I just looked at them. I didn't tell them to keep their hands on the bar, but they kept them there.

I watched all three of them. Most of all I watched Kaufman's eyes. He'd have a gun back of the bar somewhere. I watched his eyes till I knew where it was. I couldn't see it from where I stood, but I knew now just where he kept it.

I asked, "You guys want anything?"

It was the horse-faced one that answered. He said, "Not a thing, pal. Not a thing."

He turned his head to Kaufman. He said, "Nuts to you, George. For ten apiece we should play for keeps?"

I looked at Kaufman. I said, "It was a dirty trick, George. Maybe you should move up the bar a few steps."

He hesitated, and I let my hand slide another inch inside my coat.

He took three slow steps backwards.

I walked behind the bar and picked up his gun. It was a short-barrelled thirty-two revolver on a thirty-eight frame. A nice gun.

I swung out the cylinder and let the cartridges drop into dirty dishwater in one of the sinks built in back of the bar. I dropped the gun in after them.

I turned around to pick a bottle off the back bar. In the mirror I caught Uncle Ambrose's eye. He was sitting there at the table, grinning like a Cheshire cat. He winked at me.

The most expensive stuff I could see was a bottle of Teacher's Highland Cream.

"On the house, boys," I said. I poured them each a shot.

Horse-face grinned at me. He said, "You wouldn't want to

give us our ten apiece outa the register, would you, pal? I figure we got it coming, from the dirty trick George played on us."

My uncle had stood up and was strolling over to the bar. He came in between Horse-face and the big guy. He looked tiny, standing there between them.

He said, "Let me," and took out his wallet. He took out two tens and gave one to each of the men on either side of him. He said, "You're right, fellas. I wouldn't want to see you rooked on this deal."

Horse-face stuffed the bill into his pants pocket. He said, "You're a right guy, mister. We'd just as soon earn this. Like us to?"

He looked at Kaufman, and the bigger guy looked at Kaufman, too. Kaufman started to get pale, and took another step backwards.

"Nope," my uncle said. "We like George. We wouldn't want anything to happen to George. Give us another shot around, Ed."

I filled their glasses with the Highland Cream, and I put out two more shot glasses and solemnly put three-quarters of an ounce of white soda in each of them.

"Don't forget George," Uncle Ambrose said. "Maybe George will drink with us."

"Sure," I said.

I took a fifth shot glass and carefully filled it with white soda. I slid it along the bar toward Kaufman.

He didn't pick it up.

The other four of us drank.

Horse-face said, "You're sure you don't want us to—"

"Nope," my uncle said. "We like George. He's a nice guy

when you get to know him. You boys better run along now. The copper on this beat'll be along soon. He might look in."

Horse-face said, "George wouldn't squawk," and he looked at Kaufman.

We had one more drink around, and then the two muscle-boys went out. It was very chummy.

My uncle grinned at me. He said, "You ring it up for George, Ed. You poured six shots of Scotch—figure it at fifty cents a shot. And five white sodas, counting George's." He put a five-dollar bill on the bar. "Ring up three-fifty."

"Right," I said. "We wouldn't want to be obligated to George."

I rang it up and gave Uncle Ambrose a dollar and a half change. I put the five in the register.

We went back to the table and sat down.

We sat there fully five minutes before Kaufman got the idea that it was all over and that we were going to make like it never happened.

At the end of that five minutes a man came in and wanted a beer. Kaufman drew it for him.

Then he came over to our table. He was still a little green about the gills.

He said, "Honest to God, I don't know anything about this Hunter guy's getting bumped off. Just what I told at the inquest."

Neither of us said anything.

Kaufman stood there a moment, and then he went back of the bar again. He poured himself two fingers of whiskey in a tumbler and drank it. It was the first drink I'd seen him take.

We sat there, straight through, until eight-thirty that evening.

A lot of customers came and went. Kaufman didn't take another drink, but he dropped and broke two glasses.

We didn't talk much walking back over Chicago Avenue. While we were eating, my uncle said, "You did swell, Ed. I—Hell, I'll be honest; I didn't think you had it in you."

I grinned at him. I said, "I'll be honest, too. I didn't think so either. Are we going back there tonight?"

"Nope. He's softened up pretty well right now, but we'll skip it till tomorrow. We'll take it from a different tack then. And maybe by tomorrow night we'll put the screws on him."

"You're sure he isn't on the level, that he's holding back something?"

"Kid, he's scared. He was scared at the inquest. I think he knows something; anyway, he's the only lead we got right now. Look, why don't you go home and turn in early? Get some sleep for a change."

"What are you doing?"

"I'm seeing Bassett at eleven. Nothing till then."

"I'll wait and see him too. I couldn't sleep."

"Uh-huh. After-effect. You put yourself in a tight spot back there. Your hand steady?"

I nodded. I said, "But my guts are shaking like a leaf. I was scared stiff, all the time I was doing it. I leaned against the end of the bar so I wouldn't fall over."

"You're probably right about not sleeping," he said. "but there's a couple of hours between now and eleven. How do you want to kill it?"

I said, "Maybe I'll drop in the Elwood Press. I want to pick up the checks Pop and I have coming—half a week, no, better than half a week, three days is three-fifths of a week."

"Can you get them in the evening?"

"Sure, they're in the foreman's desk and the night foreman has a key. And I can get the stuff out of Pop's locker, and take it home."

"Uh-huh. And listen—there couldn't be any shop angle to your dad's being killed, could there?"

I said, "I don't see how. It's just a printing shop; I mean they don't run off any counterfeit money or anything."

"Well, keep your eyes and your brain open anyway. He have any enemies there? Everybody like him?"

"Yeah, everybody liked him. Oh, he didn't have really close friends there, but he got along all right. He and Bunny Wilson used to see a lot of each other. Not so much since Bunny got put on the night shift and Pop stayed on days. And there's Jake, the day-side foreman. He and Pop were fairly friendly."

"Uh-huh. Well, I'm meeting Bassett at the place on Grand Avenue where we saw him the other night. You be there around eleven if you want to join us."

"I'll be there," I said.

I walked around to the Elwood, on State Street up near Oak. It seemed funny to be going in there after dark, and not to be going to work.

I walked up the dimly lit stairs to the third floor and stood at the door of the composing room, looking in. There were the linotypes along the west side of the room, six of them. Bunny was setting type at the nearest one. There were operators at three of the others.

Pop's was vacant. Not because he wasn't there, I mean, but just because there are fewer operators on nights than there are machines and that one wasn't used. I stood there for a few minutes in the doorway, and nobody noticed me.

Then I saw Ray Metzner, the night foreman, walk across to his desk and I followed him and got there just as he sat down.

He looked up and said, "Hi, Ed," and I said, "Hi," back and then both of us seemed stuck for something to say.

Bunny Wilson saw me then and came walking over. He said, "Coming back to work, Ed?"

"Pretty soon," I told him.

Ray Metzner was opening the locked drawer of the desk. He found the checks and I stuck them in my pocket. He said, "You sure look like a million bucks, Ed."

I'd forgotten how I was dressed; it embarrassed me a little, here.

Bunny said, "Look, kid, when you're ready to come back, why don't you ask them to put you on the night shift instead of days? We can use you here, can't we, Ray?"

Metzner nodded. He said, "It's an idea, Ed. It's a good shift, pays a little more. And—you're learning keyboard, aren't you?"

I nodded.

He said, "You can get more practice, nights. I mean, a couple of machines are always idle. Any time it's slack and we can spare you half an hour or so, you can go over and set for practice."

"I'll think about it," I said. "Maybe I'll do it."

I saw what they meant; I'd miss Pop more on the day side, where I was used to working with him. Maybe they were right, I thought. Anyway, they were nice guys.

"Well," I said, "I'm going back to the lockers; then I guess

I'll run along. You got a master key that'll open Pop's, haven't you, Ray?"

"Sure," he said. He took it off his ring of keys and gave it to me.

Bunny said, "Fifteen minutes to lunch time, Ed. I'm going to have a sandwich and coffee down at the corner. Wait and have something with me."

"Just ate," I told him. "But, sure, I'll have a cup of Java."

Metzner said, "Go ahead now, Bunny. I'll punch your card for you. I'd join you, but I bring my lunch."

We went back to the lockers. There wasn't anything I wanted out of mine. I opened Pop's. There wasn't anything in it except an old sweater, his line-gauge, and the little black suitcase.

The sweater wasn't worth taking home, but I didn't want to throw it away. I put it and the pica stick in my own locker and took the little suitcase. It was locked, so I didn't try to open it there.

When I got home, I'd find out what was in it. I'd always been mildly curious. It was just a dime-store type of cardboard case, about four inches thick and about twelve by eighteen inches. It had stood on end at the back of his locker ever since I'd been working at Elwood with him.

I'd asked him once what was in it and he'd said, "Just some old junk of mine, Ed, I don't want to leave around home. Nothing important." He hadn't volunteered anything beyond that, and I hadn't asked again.

We went downstairs and to the little greasy spoon on the corner of State and Oak. We didn't talk much while he ate a sandwich and a piece of pie.

Then we lighted cigarettes and Bunny asked, "Have they—uh—got the guy yet? The guy that killed your dad?"

I shook my head.

"They don't—uh—They don't suspect anybody, do they, Ed?"

I looked at him.

It was such a hell of a funny way for him to say it. It took me maybe a minute to take that sentence apart and to see through it.

Then I said, "They don't suspect Mom, if that's what you mean, Bunny."

"I didn't mean—"

"Don't be a dope, Bunny. That's what you had to mean, asking it that way. Well, Mom didn't have anything to do with it."

"I know she didn't, Ed. That's what I— Oh, hell, I'm putting my foot in it worse all the time. I should have kept my trap shut completely. I haven't got brains enough to be subtle. I was trying to get information out of you without giving any, and it's going to be the other way around."

"All right, then," I said. "Give."

"Look, Ed, when a guy gets killed, they always suspect his wife unless she's in the clear. Don't make me explain why; they just do. Same when a woman's killed; they automatically suspect her husband first."

I said, "I guess maybe they would. But this was different; this was a straight holdup."

"Sure, but they'll investigate other angles, too. Just in case it isn't what it looks like, see? Well, I know where Madge—your mom—was between twelve and half past one, so she's in the clear. If she'd need an alibi, I could give her one. That's what I meant when I said I knew she didn't do it."

"Where did you see her?"

Bunny said, "I was having a drink or two Wednesday, my night off, and I called up your place about ten to see if Wally was around. And he—"

"I remember now," I said. "I answered the phone and told you he'd already gone out."

"Yeah. So I dropped in several places, thinking I might run into him. I didn't. Only about midnight I was in a place near Grand Avenue; I don't know the name of it. And Madge came in. Said she'd just decided to come down for a nightcap before she went to bed; that Wally hadn't come home yet."

I asked, "Was she mad about it, or anything?"

"I dunno, kid. She didn't seem to be, but you can't tell with a woman. Women are funny. Anyway we had a few drinks and talked, and it was about half past one when I walked her home and then went home myself. I know because I got home at a little before two o'clock."

I said, "It's a good alibi, if she needed one. Only she doesn't, Bunny. Say, was that why you came to the inquest? I wondered at the time why you were there."

"Sure. I wanted to know what time it happened. And everything. At the inquest they didn't even ask Madge whether she'd been in or out that evening. So I knew it was all right, up to then. Haven't they asked her?"

"Not that I know of," I told him. "It just didn't come up at all. I knew she'd been out, because she was still dressed that morning when I went in to wake up Pop, but—"

"Still dressed? Good Lord, Ed, why would she be—"

I wished now I'd kept my yap shut. I'd have to tell him now. I said, "She had a bottle at home and must have kept on drinking, waiting for Pop to come home. Only she went to sleep without undressing."

"Don't the cops know that?"

"I don't know, Bunny." I told him what had happened that morning. I said, "She was starting to get up when I left the place; I heard her. Well, if she changed dresses or had that one off and a bathrobe on when they came, they wouldn't know. If she answered the door the way she was when I left, well, they'd be pretty dumb if they didn't know."

"That's okay then," Bunny said. "If they don't know she was out at all, all right. If they—Well, you see what I mean."

"Sure," I said.

I was a little relieved myself, I found, to know where Mom had been that night and that there really wasn't anything to worry about.

Bunny tried again to lend me money when I left him.

When I went into the tavern, Uncle Ambrose was sitting alone in the booth we had occupied a few nights ago. It still lacked a few minutes of eleven o'clock.

He glanced at me, and then at the suitcase, and his eyes asked the question for him. I told him what it was.

He put it on the table in front of him and then started rummaging in his pockets. He came out with a paper clip and bent part of it straight, then put a little hook on the end.

"You don't mind, Ed?"

"Of course not," I told him. "Go ahead."

The lock was easy. He lifted the lid.

"I'll be damned," I said.

At first glance, it was a puzzling hodgepodge. Then one item after another began to make sense. They wouldn't have made sense to me before my uncle had told me some of the things Pop had done when he was younger.

There was a black, fuzzy wig, the kind that went with a minstrel's blackface make-up. Half a dozen bright-red balls about two and half inches in diameter, the size for juggling. A dagger, in a sheath, of Spanish workmanship. A beautifully balanced single-shot target pistol. A black mantilla. A little clay figure of an Aztec idol.

There were other things. You couldn't take them all in at a glance.

There was a sheaf of papers with handwriting on them. There was something wrapped in tissue paper. There was a battered harmonica.

It was Pop's life, I thought, stuffed into a little suitcase. Anyway, one phase of his life. They were things he'd wanted to keep, but not to keep at home where they might have been kicked around or lost, or where he might have to answer questions about them.

A sound made me look up, and Bassett was standing there looking down. "Where'd this stuff come from?" he asked.

"Sit down," my uncle told him. He'd picked up one of the bright-red juggling balls and was looking at it like a man might look into a crystal. His eyes looked kind of funny. Not crying, exactly, but kind of not quite not-crying, either.

Without looking at either me or Bassett, he said, "Tell him, kid," and I told Bassett about the suitcase and where it had been.

Bassett reached over and picked up the sheaf of papers. He turned it around and said, "I'll be damned. It's Spanish."

"Looks like poetry," I said. "The way it's divided into lines. Uncle Am, did Pop ever write poetry in Spanish?"

He nodded without taking his eyes off the red ball.

Bassett was shuffling through the stack and a smaller paper fell out. A little rectangle of new crisp paper, about three by four inches. It was a printed form, but filled in with typewriting and a scribbled signature in ink.

Bassett was sitting next to me and I read it while he did.

It was a premium receipt from an insurance company, the Central Mutual. It was dated less than two months ago and was a quarterly premium receipt on a policy in the name of Wallace Hunter.

I looked at the amount and whistled. The policy was for five thousand bucks. A little notation under "Straight Life Policy" read "Double Indemnity." Ten thousand bucks—or is murder an accidental death?

The name of the beneficiary was shown, too. Mrs. Wallace Hunter.

Bassett cleared his throat and Uncle Ambrose looked up. Bassett passed the premium receipt across the table to him.

"Afraid it's all we need," he said. "A motive. She told me he didn't carry insurance."

Uncle Ambrose read it slowly. He said, "You're crazy. Madge didn't do it."

"She was out that night. She had a motive. She's lied on two counts. I'm sorry, Hunter, but—"

The bartender was standing by the table. He asked, "What's yours, gents?"

CHAPTER 8

"LISTEN," I SAID, when the guy had taken our order and had left. "Mom couldn't have done it. She's got an alibi."

They both looked at me, and Uncle Am's left eyebrow went up half a pica.

I told them about Bunny.

I watched Bassett's face while I told it, but I couldn't tell anything. When I got done, he said, "Maybe. I'll look up the guy. Know where he lives?"

"Sure," I said. I gave him Bunny Wilson's address. "Gets off work at one-thirty in the morning. He might or might not go right home. I dunno."

"All right," he said. "I'll hold off till I talk to this Bunny guy. It might not mean anything, though. He's a friend of the family's—that means of hers, too. He could've stretched the hour a bit to do her a favor."

"Why would he?"

Bassett shrugged. The kind of a shrug that doesn't mean you don't know, but that it's nothing you want to talk about.

It told plenty. I said, "Listen, damn y—"

Uncle Am put his hand on my arm. He had a grip.

He said, "Shut up, Ed. Take yourself a walk around the block and cool down."

His grip got tight and it hurt.

He said, "Go ahead. I mean it."

Bassett got up to let me out of the booth, and I got up and went out fast. The hell with them, I thought.

I went out and walked west on Grand.

It wasn't until I started to take out a cigarette that I found I had something in my hand. It was a round, red, rubber ball. Bright shiny red, one of the half dozen that had been in the suitcase.

I stopped by the staircase leading up to the el, and stared at the ball in my hand. Something was coming back to me. A vague picture of a man juggling some of them. I'd been a baby then. He was laughing and the bright balls were flashing in the lamplight of the nursery room in the Gary flat, and I stopped crying to watch the whirling spheres.

Not once, but often. How old had I been? I remember I'd been walking, once at least, walking, reaching out for the bright balls, and he'd given me one to play with, and had laughed when I put it to my mouth to chew it.

I couldn't have been over three—not much over, anyway—the last time I'd seen them. I'd forgotten completely.

Only this ball in my hand, the size and the feel and the brightness of it, brought back the lost memory.

But the man, the juggler—I couldn't picture him at all.

Only laughter, and the bright flashing spheres.

I tossed it up and caught it, and it felt good. I wondered if I could learn to juggle six of them. I tossed it up again.

Somebody laughed and said, "Want some jacks?"

I caught the ball and put it in my pocket, and turned around.

It was Bobby Reinhart, the apprentice at Heiden's Mortuary, the guy who had identified Pop when he'd come to work on Thursday morning and found the body there. He was wearing a white Palm Beach suit that set off his darkish skin and his grease-slicked black hair.

He was grinning. It wasn't a nice grin. I didn't like it.

I said, "Did you say something?"

The grin faded out, and his face got ugly.

That was lovely. I just hoped he'd say something. I looked at his face and thought of him being with Gardie, and I thought of his having seen Pop there in the mortuary, and maybe working on his body, or watching while Heiden did, and—Oh, hell, if it had been somebody else, it would have been different. But when you don't like a guy to begin with, something like that happens, and you hate him.

He said, "What the hell are you getting—?" And he was reaching his right hand into the side pocket of his Palm Beach coat.

Maybe he was reaching for a cigarette; I didn't know. He'd hardly have been reaching for a gun, out here in the open, even if there was nobody within half a block. But I didn't wait to find out. Maybe I was just looking for an excuse.

I grabbed him by the shoulder and whirled him around, and I had hold of his right wrist from behind, twisting it. He made a noise that was half-cursing, half-squawking, and something hit the concrete with a metallic clink.

I let go of his wrist and got the back of the collar of his coat. I jerked to keep him from stooping down, and as our shadows got out of the way, I could see the thing on the sidewalk was a set of brass knucks.

He gave a hell of a hard lunge to get away and the cloth of

the coat tore in my hands. It ripped all the way down the back, and the right side of what was left of it fell down from his shoulder, and a notebook and a billfold fell out of the inside pocket.

He was backed up against the building now, and he looked undecided. He wanted to take me apart, I could tell, but without those brass knucks, he knew he couldn't do it. And that torn coat was in his way.

He stood there, panting, ready if I came for him, not daring to try to pick up the things that had fallen from his coat, not willing to run away without them.

I gave the knucks a kick that sent them halfway across the street, and then took a step back. I said, "Okay, pick up your marbles and scram. Open your yap and I'll knock your teeth out."

His eyes said plenty, but his mouth didn't dare to. He came forward to get the stuff, and I looked down at it, and said, "*Wait a minute,*" and reached down and picked up the billfold before he did.

It was Pop's wallet.

It was tooled leather, a nice one, and almost new. But there was a diagonal scratch across the polished leather. That scratch had been from the sharp corner of a hard-metal linotype slug. The wallet had happened to be lying on Pop's stand at the lino, and he'd let some slugs slide off a galley onto it. I'd been there.

I heard a car swinging in to the curb, and Bobby took a look past me and started running. I started after him, shoving the wallet into my pocket. A voice yelled, "Hey—" The car started up again.

I caught him as he was trying to cut through a vacant lot, and was beating the hell out of him when the car and the squad coppers got there, and one of them got each of us. One caught my coat from in back, pulled me away from Bobby Reinhart, and slammed me alongside the face with the flat of his hand.

"Break it up, punks," he said. "Down to the station for you."

I wanted to kick out backward, but that wouldn't do any good.

I gulped air as we were headed for the squad car, until I had enough of my mind back to talk, and then I started to talk fast.

"This isn't just a fight," I said. "This is part of a murder case. Bassett of Homicide is in a tavern two blocks east of here. Take us there; Bassett'll want this guy."

The copper that had me was running his hands over the outside of my pockets. He said, "Tell it down at the station."

The other one said, "There's a Homicide dick named Bassett. What case is it, kid?"

"My father," I said. "Wallace Hunter. Killed in an alley off Franklin Street last week."

He said, "There *was* a guy killed there." He looked at the copper that had me, and shrugged. He said, "We can look there. Two blocks. If it *is* a homicide case—"

We got in the car, and they didn't take any chances on us. They collared us again when they marched us into the tavern. It made quite a parade.

Bassett and Uncle Am were still in the booth. They looked up, and neither of them showed any surprise.

The copper who knew Bassett beat me to the punch. He said, "We found these punks fighting. This one said you'd be interested. Are you?"

Bassett said, "I could be. You can let go of him, anyway. What is it, Ed?"

I took the wallet out of my pocket and tossed it on the table of the booth. I said, "Pop's wallet. This son of a bitch had it."

Bassett picked up the wallet and opened it. There were a few bills in it. One five and several singles. He looked at the identification card under the celluloid and then looked up at Bobby.

"Where'd you get it, Reinhart?" His voice was very mild and calm.

"Gardie Hunter. She gave it to me."

I heard Uncle Am let out a long breath that he'd been holding. He didn't look up at me. He kept his eyes on the wallet in Bassett's hand.

Bassett asked, "When was this?"

"Last night. Sure it had been her old man's. She said so."

Bassett folded the wallet back shut and put it carefully into his pocket. He took out a cigarette and lighted it.

Then he nodded to the squad-car men. He said, "Thanks a lot, boys. Look, I'd sort of like to keep track of Bobby here till I can check that story. Will you take him and book him on disorderly?"

"Okay."

"Who's on the desk tonight?"

"Norwald."

Bassett nodded. "I know him. Tell him I'll probably phone in pretty soon and tell him he can let Reinhart go." He took out the wallet again and handed Bobby the bills and identification from it. He said, "I guess we won't need these, son. The wallet's evidence, for a while."

Bobby looked around at me when they were taking him to the door.

I said, "Any time. Any place."

They took him out.

Bassett stood up. He said to Uncle Am, "Well, it was a nice try."

Uncle Am said, "You know it doesn't mean anything. About that wallet."

Bassett shrugged.

He turned to me. "Kid, 'fraid you can't sleep home tonight. You can bunk with your uncle, can't you?"

"Why?" I asked.

"We'll have to do something we should have done right away. Search the place. For the insurance policy, and anything else we might find."

Uncle Am nodded. "He can stay with me."

Bassett went out. Uncle Am sat there and didn't say anything.

I said, "I guess I went off kind of half-cocked. I threw a monkey wrench in things."

He turned and looked at me. He said, "You look like hell. Go wash your face and straighten yourself out. I think you're going to have a mouse, too."

I said, "You ought to see the other guy."

That got a snort out of him, and I knew it was going to be all right with him. I went back to the washroom and cleaned up.

He asked, "How do you feel?"

"About that high," I said.

"I mean physically. Can you stay up all night?"

"If I can get up, I can stay up."

He said, "We've been piddling along. We've been kidding ourselves we've been investigating. We've been babes in the woods. We'd better start chopping down some trees."

"Swell," I said. "What's Bassett going to do—arrest Mom?"

"He's going to take her in for questioning. Gardie, too, now that wallet business came up. I had him talked out of it; he was going to give us another few days to crack Kaufman."

"He'll let them go when he's questioned them?"

"I don't know, kid. I don't know. If he finds that policy, maybe he won't. We got two kicks in the teeth tonight—that insurance receipt and the wallet. They both point the wrong way, but try to tell that to Bassett."

I had the red rubber ball in my hand again, playing with it. He reached over and took it from me and started squeezing it. Each time, it went almost flat. He had tremendously strong hands.

He said, "I wish we'd never found this stuff. It—Oh, hell, I can't explain. I just wish Wally hadn't kept it."

I said, "I think I know what you mean."

"He must have been a hell of a mess, Ed. I hadn't seen him in ten years. My God, what can happen to a guy in ten years—"

"Listen, Uncle Am," I said, "is there any way he could have done it himself? Hit himself with—say, with one of the bottles? Or—this sounds screwy except that he used, you said, to juggle Indian clubs—thrown it up high and stood under it when it came down? I know it sounds crazy, but—"

"It doesn't, kid, except for one thing you don't know: Wally couldn't have killed himself. He had a—well, not exactly a phobia, but maybe you could call it a psychic block. He couldn't have killed himself. It wasn't fear of death—he might have wanted to die. I remember once when he did."

I said, "I don't see how you can be sure. Maybe he didn't want to badly enough, then."

He said, "It was on our trip through Mexico, south of Chihuahua. He was bitten by a Cugulla adder. We were alone, on a lonely road across wild country, not much more than a trail. We didn't have any first-aid stuff, and it wouldn't have mattered if we had. There isn't any antidote for a Cugulla bite. You die within two hours, and it's one of the worst and most painful deaths there is. It's unadulterated hell.

"His leg started swelling and hurting like hell right away. He had the only gun between us, and we—well, we said so long, and he tried to shoot himself. He simply couldn't—his reflexes wouldn't work. He begged me to do it. I—I don't know; I might have if it had got much worse, but we heard someone coming. It was a mestizo, riding an ancient burro.

"He said the snake wasn't a Cugulla—we'd shot it and it was lying there in the road. It was a local species that looked almost exactly like a Cugulla. And it was poisonous all right, but nothing like the real McCoy. We got Wally tied on the burro and packed him three miles to a medico in the next village, and we saved him, or the medico did."

I said, "But—"

"We had to stay there a month. That doc was a swell guy. I worked for him to help pay for us staying there while Wally was getting better, but evenings I read his books—mostly the ones on psychology and psychiatry. He had a flock of 'em, in English and Spanish.

"That's where I picked up a good start on what I know about stuff like that, and I've read a lot since—besides the practical angles you get working a mitt-camp. But, kid, we sort of psychoanalyzed Wally and he had it. There are people who couldn't kill themselves—it's a physical and mental impossibility, no matter what. It's not too common, but it's not too rare either. It's an anti-suicide psychosis. And it's not something that would wear off or change as he got older."

I asked, "That's straight; you're not kidding me?"

"Not on any of it, kid."

He squeezed the rubber ball some more.

He said, "Kid, when we go in, you lean against the inside of the door. Don't say anything at all."

"Go in where?"

"Kaufman's room. He isn't married; he lives in a rooming house on LaSalle Street, a little north of Oak. He walks home. I've been there and I know the layout. We've monkeyed around with him too long. We'll write him off our books tonight, before things get too cold."

"Okay," I said. "When do we start?"

"He closes fairly early Monday night. Any time after one, he might get there. We'll have to leave pretty soon; it's after midnight now."

We had another drink, and then we left. We went by the Wacker and left Pop's suitcase there. Then we went north on Clark to Oak, and over to LaSalle.

My uncle picked a deep doorway on the west side of LaSalle, just north of the corner, and we stood in there and waited. We waited almost an hour and only a few people went by.

Then Kaufman passed us. He didn't look in the doorway.

We waited till he was just past, and then stepped out and went up alongside him, one of us on either side.

He stopped as abruptly as if he'd run into a wall, but, one of us holding each of his arms, we started him walking again. I took a look at his face, and then didn't look again. It wasn't nice to look at. It was the face of a man who thinks he is dead, and who doesn't like it. It was just the color of the sidewalk under our feet.

He said, "Listen, you guys, I—"

"We'll talk in your room," my uncle said.

We reached the doorway.

Uncle Ambrose let go of Kaufman's arm and went in first. He walked confidently down the hallway as though he knew where he was going. I remembered he said he'd been here before.

I walked third, behind Kaufman. Halfway down the hall, he lagged a bit. I touched the small of his back lightly with the end of my index finger and he jumped. He almost crowded Uncle Am, going up the stairs.

On the third floor, my uncle took a key from his pocket and opened the door of a room. He went on in and flicked the light.

We followed him, and I closed the door and leaned against it.

My part in this was over, except for leaning against that door.

Kaufman said, "Listen, damn it, I—"

"Be quiet," my uncle told him. "Sit down." He gave the tavern keeper a very light push that sent him to a sitting position on the edge of the bed.

My uncle paid no more attention to him. He walked over to the dresser by the window. He reached around the end of it and pulled the window shade down flush with the sill.

Then he picked up the alarm clock on the dresser. It ticked loudly; the hands stood at nine minutes of two. He looked at his own wrist watch and adjusted the time to a quarter of two. He gave each of the winding keys a few turns and then turned the button that turned the alarm hand. He set it for two o'clock, pulled up the little lever that turned it on.

"Nice clock you have there," he said. "Hope it won't bother your neighbors if it goes off at two. We have to catch a train."

He opened the top left dresser drawer and reached in. His hand came out holding a little nickel-plated thirty-two revolver.

He said, "You won't mind if we borrow this a moment, will you, George?" He looked across the room at me. "Dangerous things, guns, kid. I've never owned one and never will. They get you in trouble faster'n anything."

"Yeah," I said.

He spun the cylinder, broke the gun, and snapped it shut. He said, "Kid, throw me that pillow."

I took the pillow from the bed and tossed it to him.

He held the gun in his right hand and bent the pillow around it with his left.

He leaned back against the dresser.

The clock ticked.

Kaufman was sweating. There were big drops on his forehead. He said, "You guys can't get away with this."

"With what?" my uncle asked him. He looked at me and grinned. He said, "Kid, you got any idea what this guy is talking about?"

I said, "Maybe he thinks we're threatening him."

My uncle looked surprised. "Why, we wouldn't do that. We like George."

The clock ticked again.

Kaufman took a handkerchief out of his pocket and wiped his forehead.

He said, "All right, shut that goddam alarm off. What do you want to know?"

I saw some of the tension go out of Uncle Am; I hadn't realized it was there until it left him. He said, "You know what we want to know, pal. Just tell it your own way."

"Does the name Harry Reynolds mean anything to you?"

Uncle Am said, "Just keep talking. It will."

"Harry Reynolds is a hood. He's dynamite. Three weeks ago he was in my place, sitting at the back with a couple guys, when this Wally Hunter comes in for a drink. There are a couple guys with Hunter, too."

"What kind of guys?"

"Just ordinary guys. Printers. A fat one and a little one. One I didn't know, but Hunter called him Jay. The other one had been in with Hunter before; his name is Bunny."

My uncle glanced at me, and I nodded. I knew who Jay would be.

Kaufman said, "They had just a drink around, and left, and one of the guys with Reynolds got up and left right after them, like he was going to follow them. Then this Reynolds comes over to the bar and asks me what the name of the guy who stood in the middle of the three of them was. I told him Wally Hunter."

My uncle asked, "Did he recognize the name?"

"Yeah. I got it he hadn't been sure till I told him the name and then he was sure, all right. He asks me where this Hunter lives, and I say I don't know—which was the truth. He came in once in a while, maybe once a week, but I didn't know where he lived.

"So he lets it go at that, has a few more drinks and they leave.

"The next day he comes back. He says he wants to get in touch with Hunter about something and next time he comes in I should find out where he lives. And he gives me a phone number, too, and says the minute Hunter comes in I should call that number and say Hunter's there—but I shouldn't say anything to Hunter about it."

"What was the phone number?"

Kaufman said, "Wentworth three-eight-four-two. I was to leave a message if he wasn't there. Same if I found out Hunter's address from him; I was to call that number and leave the message."

"You say this was the next day?"

Kaufman nodded. He said, "I take it he sent one of the boys to follow Hunter home, but he lost him. So Reynolds came back to get it through me. He let me know what'd happen if I didn't—if he found out Hunter had been back and I hadn't let him know."

Uncle Am asked, "Did this Hunter come in again between that night and the night he was killed?"

"Nope, he didn't come in for two weeks after that. Till the night he was killed. And that night everything happened like I told at the inquest except that I called the number. Hell, I had to. Reynolds would've killed me if I hadn't."

"You talked to Reynolds personally?"

"No, nobody answered the phone when I called that number. I called twice, once a couple minutes after Hunter came in, and again ten minutes after that. Nobody answered. I was damn glad. I didn't want to get mixed up in it any more'n I had to to keep Reynolds from burning me down. What's your angle in this?"

Uncle Am said, "Don't worry about our angle. We won't get you in trouble with Reynolds. What'd you tell Reynolds when you saw him?"

"I didn't see him since. He never came around. Hell, he wouldn't. He got in touch with Hunter some other way. He— or one of his boys—must've been following Hunter that night, waiting outside while he was in here. He must've been—"

The alarm went off and all three of us jumped. Uncle Am reached behind him and shut it off. He tossed the pillow back on the bed and put the little thirty-two on top of the dresser.

He asked, "Where does Harry Reynolds live?"

"I don't know. All I know is that phone number. Wentworth three-eight-four-two."

"What's his line?"

"Big-time stuff only. Banks, pay rolls, stuff like that. His brother's in stir, doing life, for a bank job."

My uncle shook his head sadly. He said, "George, you shouldn't get mixed up with people like that. Who were the other lugs who were with Reynolds the night he was in your place last—the night Wally Hunter came in?"

"One was called Dutch. A big guy. The other one was a little wop torpedo; I don't know his name. Dutch was the one followed Hunter out and lost him—I guess he lost him, or Reynolds wouldn't had to come back the next day."

My uncle said, "That's all you can tell us, George? Now you've gone this far, the more the merrier—if you get what I mean."

Kaufman said, "I get what you mean. If I knew any more I'd tell you, all right. I hope you find him, now. You got a phone number. Just don't tell him where you got it."

"We won't, George. We won't tell anybody. We'll go now, and let you go to sleep." He started to the door, and I turned the knob to open it. He turned back to Kaufman a moment.

He said, "Listen, George, I'm pretending to play along with the cops on this; I may have to give them something. They can find Reynolds easier than we can if the phone number is a bust. But you keep that phone number under your hat. If Bassett comes around to see you, give him everything you gave me except the phone number. You were just to get Hunter's address, and Reynolds would come back for it. Only he didn't."

We went out and down the stairs, out into the clean night air.

I thought, we have a name now. We know who we're looking for. We got a name and a phone number. And this time we were up against the big-time. Hoods; not mugs like Kaufman.

And we were going it by ourselves; Uncle Am wasn't giving Bassett that phone number.

Under the street light on Oak Street, Uncle Am looked at me. He asked, "Scared, kid?"

My throat was a little dry. I nodded.

He said, "So am I. Scared spitless. Shall we level with Bassett or shall we have some fun?"

I said, "Let's—try the fun."

CHAPTER 9

THE COOL NIGHT AIR felt swell now. I'd been sweating. My collar felt tight and I loosened it and shoved my hat back on my head.

It was reaction again, but a different kind of reaction. I felt taller. I wasn't jittery, like after the tight we'd been in at the tavern.

We walked south on Wells Street and we didn't say anything. We didn't have to. Somehow after what had happened, Uncle Am was a part of me and I was a part of him.

And I remembered that phrase again—*we're the Hunters*—and I thought, we're going to do it. The cops can't, but we can. I knew then that I hadn't really believed it before. I believed it now. I knew it now.

I was scared, yes, but it was a nice kind of afraidness—like when you read a good ghost story and it makes prickles run up and down your spine, but makes you like them.

We cut east on Chicago Avenue, and we went past the police station with the two blue lights by the door. I looked up the steps as we walked past it, and I didn't feel so good any more. Mom and Gardie would be having a tough time in there. Or had they taken them to the Homicide Bureau downtown?

But Mom hadn't done it. Bassett was way off on that.

We rounded the corner to Clark Street. Uncle Am asked, "Cup coffee, kid?"

"Sure," I said. "But are we going to call that number tonight? It's getting later."

"From now on it gets earlier," he said. "A few minutes won't matter."

We ordered a bowl of chili and coffee apiece, in the joint just north of Superior. We had our end of the counter to ourselves; two loud-voiced women down near the other end were arguing about somebody named Carey.

The chili was good, but it didn't taste good. I kept thinking about Mom. I thought, anyway they don't use a rubber hose on women.

Uncle Am said, "Think about something else, Ed."

"Sure. What?"

"Anything. What the hell." He looked around and his eye lit on the handbag one of the women had lying on the counter. "Think about handbags. Ever think about handbags?"

"No," I said. "Why should I?"

"Suppose you were a leather-goods designer. Then you'd be plenty interested. What's a handbag for? It's a substitute for pockets, that's all. A man has pockets, and a woman hasn't. Why? Because pockets—loaded ones—would spoil a woman's shape. She'd bulge in the wrong places, or too much in the right places. Wouldn't she?"

"I guess so," I said.

"Why, take handkerchiefs. Women do carry handkerchiefs in pockets sometimes, but little tiny ones, while a man carries big ones. And it isn't because they have any less snot in their noses than men do; it's because a big handkerchief would make a bulge. If they did carry big handkerchiefs, they'd carry them in pairs. But let's get back to handbags."

"Sure," I said. "Let's get back to handbags."

"The more a handbag holds the better it is, and the smaller it looks, the better it is. Now, how would you design a handbag that would be big and look little? That would make a woman say, 'Golly, this bag holds more than you'd think'?"

"I don't know. How?"

"I think the approach would be empirical. You'd design a lot of 'em just for looks and wait till you heard a woman say one of them holds more than you'd think. Then you'd study it to see why, and try to put the same thing in other bags. You might even reduce it to an equation. You know algebra, Ed?"

"Not intimately," I told him, "and the hell with handbags. They make me think of wallets. Was Bobby Reinhart telling the truth about Gardie giving it to him?"

"Sure, kid. If he was lying, he wouldn't tell one that could be checked on that easy. He'd say he found it, or something. But don't let it worry you."

"It does, though."

"My God, why? You don't think Gardie killed him, took the wallet and then gave it to Bobby, do you? Or that Madge killed him, left the wallet lying around loose, or gave it to Gardie, do you?"

I said, "I know neither of them did it, but it looks damn bad. How *did* Gardie get the wallet?"

"He didn't take it with him, that's all. Lots of guys leave their wallets home when they go out on a bender. They stick a few bucks in their pockets and leave their wallets safe at home. Gardie found it and glommed onto the money in it, and didn't say anything. Even then it was dumb for her to give the wallet away—but if it was anything worse than that, she wouldn't have taken the chance. She'd have put the wallet in the incinerator."

"She should have, anyway," I said. "She's pretty damn dumb."

Uncle Am said, "I'm not so sure, kid. She'll get what she wants out of life. Most people do. Not all of them, but most people."

"Pop didn't," I said.

"No," Uncle Am said, "Wally didn't." He spoke slowly, as though he were choosing his words one at a time. "But there's a difference. Gardie is selfish; she won't mess up her life for the same reason Wally messed up his. If she marries the wrong guy, she'd just walk out on him.

"Wally was the kind of guy who was loyal, kid, even to lost causes. He was also the kind of guy who should never have married at all. But your mother was a real woman, Ed, and he was happy with her. And she died before he got too restless, if you know what I mean. And Madge caught him on the rebound."

I said, "Mom is—oh, skip it." I realized that I was going to stick up for her just out of loyalty. If I thought back about Mom and Pop, I remembered things, and Uncle Am was right. I was being soft, because she was in trouble now, and because she'd been different—a lot different—since Pop had died. But I shouldn't kid myself that would last.

Mom had been poison to him, and she'd have been poison to any man as decent as Pop was. Or had been, before she drove him to drink. And even his drinking had been quiet and not ever quarrelsome.

I finished my chili and pushed the bowl aside.

Uncle Am said, "Not yet, kid. Let's have another cup of coffee." He ordered them. He said, "I'm trying to think out how to handle talking to that phone number. I think best when I'm talking about something else. Let's talk about something else."

"Ladies' handbags?" I suggested.

He laughed. "They bored you, huh? Kid, that's because you don't know anything about them. The more you know about something, anything, the more interesting it is. I knew a leather-goods worker once; he could talk about handbags all night. Like a carney could talk about carnivals."

"Go ahead," I said. "I'd rather hear about carneys than about handbags. What's a blow?"

"Short for blow-off. It's a show for inside money, usually inside a freak show. I mean, say, you pay two bits to get into the freak show, and the spieler takes you around the platforms and then starts an inside bally for another two bits or more to see a special show on the inside, down at one end of the top. Why?"

I said, "I remember back at the carney you asked Hoagy to take over your ball game. He said he was sloughed and if Jake got a chance to use the blow after Springfield, he could get a cooch. What was he talking about?"

Uncle Am laughed. "You got a memory, kid."

"Yeah," I said. "I remember something out of tonight's talking, too. Wentworth three-eight-four-two. Have you got an angle yet?"

"Any minute now. Back to Hoagy. Hoagy's a sex spieler. The bally for the inside money at the freak-show top is a sex lecture with living models, for men only. Two bits each and money back if they're not satisfied."

"What do you mean, living models?" I asked.

"That's what pulls in the mooches. They want to know, too. Oh, he's got a nice spiel—but you could read it in any book on what a young man should know. And he does use living models, a couple girls in bathing suits. Discusses what types they are, as a reason for having them on the platform."

"Don't the mooches want their money back?"

"A few, a darned few. They get it, and so what? On a good night, he'll still take in a hundred bucks up and over the nut."

"What's the nut?"

"The overhead, kid. Say your expenses on a concession run thirty bucks a day; well, you're on the nut until you've taken in that much. The rest of it is profit; you're off the nut."

I drank the last of my coffee. I asked, "Why would a bank-robber have been looking for Pop?"

"I don't know, kid. We'll have to find out." He sighed and stood up. "Come on; let's start."

We walked down Clark Street to the Wacker and went up to his room.

He moved the chair out from the wall before he sat down. He said, "Stand behind me, Ed, and put your ear down to the receiver. I'll hold it a little out from my ear, and you can hear as well as I can. Use that memory of yours on what's said."

"Okay," I said. "What's the angle?"

"The hell with it. I'll ad lib. What I say depends on what they say."

"What if they say 'Hello'?" I asked him.

He chuckled. "I never thought of that. I'll wait and see."

He picked up the receiver and when he gave the number to the operator, his voice was different. It was low-pitched, gruff, with a completely different intonation. But I'd heard it before somewhere. It puzzled me for a second and then I placed it. He was imitating Hoagy's voice; we'd been talking about Hoagy and that had been the first voice he'd thought of to imitate. It was perfect.

I heard them ringing the number. I leaned closer, resting my weight on the chair back to put my ear as near the end of the receiver as I could.

It rang about three times and then a woman's voice said, "Hello."

It's funny, sometimes, how much you can tell—or anyway, guess—from a voice. Just one word, but you knew she was young, that she was pretty, and that she was smart. In all the senses of the word "smart." And just from the way she said that one word, you liked her.

My uncle said, "Who zis?"

"Claire. Wentworth three-eight-four-two."

"Howya, baby?" my uncle asked. "'Member me? This's Sammy." He sounded very drunk.

"Afraid I don't," said the voice. It was considerably cooler now. "Sammy who?"

"G'wan, you r'member me," Uncle Am said. "*Sammy*. In at the bar th'other night. Look, Claire, I know 'sawful late to call you, 'nall that, but, honey, I jus' cleaned up a crap game. Took th' boys for two G's, an' it's burning a hole. Wanta see th' town, Chez Paree, the Medoc Club, n'everywhere. Want th' prettiest gal in Chi with me. Nothin' too good. Might even buy 'er a fur coat if she likes rabbit fur. How's 'bout can I come out 'n' getcha in a cab an' we'll go—"

"No," said the voice. The receiver clicked.

"Damn," said my uncle.

"It was a good try," I told him.

He put the receiver back on the phone. He said, "They don't pay off any more on good tries. Guess I'm not so hot as a Romeo. I should've let you try."

"Me? Lord, I don't know anything about women."

"That's what I mean. Hell, kid, you could have any woman you want. Take a look in the mirror."

I laughed, but I turned around to the mirror over the dresser. I said, "I *am* getting a shiner. Damn Bobby Reinhart."

Uncle Am grinned at me in the mirror. He said, "On you it looks romantic. Save it; don't put a steak on it. Well, now we try something that won't work."

He dialed a number and asked for the Wentworth exchange clerk. He asked her for the listing on three-eight-four-two. He waited a minute and then put the receiver down with an "Okay, thanks," that sounded discouraged.

"Unlisted number," he told me. "I thought it would be."

"So what do we do now?"

He sighed. "Work from the other end. Find out what's known about this Harry Reynolds. Bassett'll know something about him, or be able to dig it out of the morgue. Only thing is, I was hoping that phone number would give us an up on Bassett. Well, tomorrow we can try a couple more razzle-dazzles. We can be a phone-quiz radio program giving a hundred-buck prize to whoever answers a phone number picked at random if he can tell us the capital of Illinois and his address. Or we can be—"

"Listen," I said, "I can get the listing on that phone number for you."

"Huh? How, kid? Those unlisted numbers are hard to get."

"Bunny Wilson's sister-in-law, his brother's wife, works for the phone company, in the office where they handle those numbers. He found out one for Jake, the foreman at the plant, once. Just so we don't get his sister-in-law in trouble for it, he can get it for us."

"Kid, that's great. How soon could we get it?"

"If I can find Bunny tonight," I told him, "we can have it by tomorrow noon, I think. He could see his sister-in-law before she goes to work; then she could phone him when she goes out to lunch. She couldn't call from work, about that."

"Bunny got a phone?"

"His landlady has—but he can use it only daytimes. I can go over there, though. He lives on Halsted Street."

"He's home from work by now?"

"He should be. If he isn't, I'll wait."

"Okay, kid. We'll split up for a while, then. Here's ten bucks. Give it to Bunny to give his sister-in-law to buy herself a new hat or something. I'm going to hunt up Bassett and find out what gives on the inquisition. He'll go easier when I tell him we blew Kaufman open. Or maybe he's convinced by now that he was on the wrong street."

"Where'll we meet?"

"Come back here. I'll tell the desk clerk to give you my key if I'm not in. You run along; I'll try to find out where Bassett is by phone before I go chasing after him."

I walked down to Grand, and was lucky enough to see an owl car coming, so it was only a few minutes before I got to Halsted and walked south to the place where Bunny roomed.

His light was off, which meant he was either out or asleep, but I went upstairs anyway. This was important enough to wake him up about.

He was out; I knocked till I was sure.

I sat down on the stairs to wait, and then I remembered that he was usually careless about locking his door, and sure enough it was unlocked. So I went in and found a magazine to read.

When it got to be four o'clock I made coffee in his little kitchenette. I made it plenty strong.

He came home, stumbling up the stairs, just as I got the coffee made. He wasn't *too* drunk, just an edge on. But I got two cups of coffee down him before I told him what I wanted. I didn't give him the whole story, but enough of it that he knew why we needed the listing on that phone number.

He said, "Sure, Ed, sure. And t'hell with the ten bucks. She owes me a few favors."

I stuck it in his pocket and told him to give it to her anyway.

"Can you talk to her before she goes to work this morning?" I asked him.

"Sure, easy. She lives way out—gets up at five-thirty. I'll stay awake till I can phone her then. Then I'll set my alarm for eleven so I'll be awake when she phones me back. You can phone me any time after noon—I'll stick around till you do."

"That's swell, Bunny. Thanks."

"Skip it. You going home now?"

"Back to the Wacker."

"I'll walk part way with you." He looked at the clock. "Then by time I get back here, it'll be time for me to phone from the all-night drugstore on the corner."

We walked over Grand Avenue, over the bridge.

He said, "You're different lately, Ed. What's changed about you? You're different."

"I don't know," I said. "Maybe it's the new suit."

"Nope. Maybe you grew up, or something. Whatever it is, I like it. I—I think you could go places, Ed, if you want to. Not get stuck in a rut, like I am."

"You're not in a rut," I said. "I thought you were going to have a shop of your own."

"I don't know, Ed. Equipment costs like hell. I got a little saved, yeah, but when I think what it takes—Hell, if I had sense enough to stay sober I could save more, but I haven't. Here I am forty, and I got maybe half enough saved up for what I want to do. Rate I'm going, I'll be old before I even get started."

He laughed a little, bitterly. "Sometimes I feel like finding one of these big-time gambling games you hear about, where there's no limit, and betting my little bankroll on one blackjack hand, quit win or lose. Then either I'd have enough, or nothing. And nothing wouldn't be much worse than half enough. Maybe better."

"Better, how?"

"Then I could quit worrying about it. Then every time I spent a quarter for a shot of whiskey or a dime for a glass of beer, it wouldn't hurt me. I'm not worried about going to hell, Ed, but I begrudge the money the ticket costs."

We walked in silence a little while and then he said, "It's my own fault, Ed. I got no kick coming, really. A guy can have anything he wants; damn near, if he wants it bad enough, if he's willing to give up other things to get it. Hell, on my income, and living alone, I could save thirty bucks a week, easy. I could have had enough money years ago. But I wanted fun out of life, too. Well, I've had it, so what the hell am I squawking about?"

We were almost to the el now, and he said, "Well, guess I'll turn back here."

We stopped walking. I said, "Come up to the flat some afternoon, Bunny, or your next evening off. Mom—Mom hasn't got many friends. She'll be glad to see you."

"I'll do that, Ed. Thanks. Uh—say, how about having one drink with me? Across the street there."

I thought a minute, and then I said, "Sure, Bunny."

I didn't want the drink, really, but I could feel that, for some obscure reason, he really wanted me to drink with him. There was something in the way he said it.

We had it, just one, and then we parted in front of the tavern. I crossed over under the el and walked toward Clark Street.

I got to wondering about Mom and Gardie, whether they were home or not, so I turned north on Franklin and then cut through the alley back of our flat. When I got into the alley I could see our kitchen windows, and there was a light on in the kitchen.

I didn't know whether it was the police, still searching, or Mom home again, so I stood there and watched awhile until I saw Mom cross the window. She was still dressed, so I knew she hadn't been home long. I saw Gardie, too. Mom was going to and from the stove, and I guess they'd just got home and were getting something to eat before they turned in.

I didn't want to go upstairs. Bassett would have told Mom I was staying with Uncle Am and she wouldn't be wondering about me. She'd worry, maybe, if she knew I was still chasing around.

I walked on through the alley and over to Clark Street. The sky was turning light with dawn.

At the Wacker, I asked the desk clerk if a key had been left for me. It hadn't been, so I knew Uncle Am was back.

Bassett was there with him. They'd swung out the writing table so one of them could sit on each side of it and they were playing cards. There was a bottle on the table between them. Bassett's eyes looked glassy.

Uncle Am asked, "Feel better with the tummy full, kid?"

I knew he was tipping me off what he'd told Bassett about where I was, so I knew the phone number was still a secret.

I said, "I ate three breakfasts. I'm set for all day now."

"Gin rummy," Uncle Am said. "Penny a point, so be quiet."

I sat down on the edge of the bed and watched the game. Uncle Am was winning; he had a lead of thirty points and two boxes. I looked at the paper they were scoring on and saw it was their third game; Uncle Am had taken the first two.

But Bassett won that hand. He took a long pull out of the bottle and turned around to face me while Uncle Am dealt the next hand. His eyes were owlishly wide. He said, "Ed, that sister of yours—somebody oughta—"

"Pick up your hand, Frank," my uncle said. "Let's get the game over with. I'll bring Ed up to date later."

Bassett picked up his cards. He dropped one of them and I got it for him. He finally got his hand arranged and took another pull at the bottle. It was a quart, and it was almost empty.

Bassett won that hand, too, but Uncle Am went gin on the next one and that put him over a hundred, and out.

Bassett said, "That's enough. Add 'em up. Jeez, I'm tired." He reached for his wallet.

Uncle Am said, "Skip it. It's about ten bucks for the three games; add 'em onto the expense account. Look, Frank, I'm going to get something to eat now. Whyn't you rest awhile? Ed might as well go home. When I get back, if you've gone to sleep, I'll wake you up."

Bassett's eyes were plenty glassy now, and half shut. All of a sudden the whiskey was hitting him, and he was very drunk. He sat on the edge of the bed, swaying.

My uncle put the table back where it belonged. He looked at Bassett and grinned, and then gave him a slight push on his left shoulder. Bassett fell back and sideways and his head landed on the pillow.

Uncle Am picked up his feet and put them on the bed, too.

He untied Bassett's shoes and took them off. He took off Bassett's shell-rimmed glasses and his hat and put them on the dresser. He loosened the detective's tie and opened the button at the collar of his shirt.

Bassett opened his eyes then. He said, "You son of a bitch."

"Sure," said my uncle, soothingly. "Sure, Frank."

We turned off the light and went out.

Going down in the elevator, I told him about Bunny and the phone number and that we could get the listing any time after noon.

He nodded. He said, "Bassett knows we're holding out something on him. He's a smart boy. I wouldn't put it past him to go see Kaufman himself and turn on a little heat."

I said, "You had Kaufman plenty scared. It'll take a bit of heat to crack him again. I think he's more scared of us now than he was of this Harry Reynolds." I thought a minute, then asked, "Say, what would we have done if that alarm clock *had* gone off before he broke?"

Uncle Am shrugged. "Looked pretty silly, I guess. How's about some breakfast—for real?"

"I could eat a cow," I told him.

We went to Thompson's at Clark and Chicago, and while we got outside ham and eggs, he told me what he'd learned from Bassett.

Gardie had admitted giving the billfold to the Reinhart boy. Her explanation had been just about what Uncle Am had suggested. Pop had an extra wallet—an old one. I'd known that. What I'd not known, and Gardie *had* known was that recently, whenever he'd gone out drinking, he'd left his good wallet and part of his money at home. He'd dropped it back of a row of books in the bookcase, and had taken only part of his money, in the old wallet.

I said, "I guess that would date from the time he got held up before. He lost his social security card and union card and everything and a good billfold. I guess he figured if he got held up again, or his pocket picked, he wouldn't lose anything but the money. It's plenty easy, I guess, to get rolled on Clark Street."

"Yeah," said Uncle Am. "Anyway, Gardie'd seen him hide the wallet once, and knew about it. So she looked, and it was there in the bookcase, with twenty bucks left in it. She figured it wouldn't hurt anybody if she kept it."

I said, "Finders' keepers, sure. I don't mind that, that's what I figure she'd do, but why did she have to give the billfold away— and make me make a damn fool of myself? Oh, well, skip it. It was an off chance that I happened to see the billfold Reinhart was carrying. Did Bassett believe her?"

"After he'd looked in the bookcase. There was dust back of the books, and marks in the dust where the billfold had been, just where she'd said."

"And—about Mom?"

"I guess he pretty well convinced himself she didn't do it, kid. Even before I got hold of him and told him about the Reynolds angle. Also they searched the flat pretty thoroughly. They didn't find any insurance policy, or anything else of interest."

"What did Bassett know about Reynolds, if anything?"

"He knew *of* him. There is such a guy, and everything Kaufman told us about him fits with what Bassett knows. Bassett thinks there's a pick-up order out for the three of them— Harry Reynolds, Dutch, and the wop torpedo. Bassett'll look into it and get their names and histories. He thinks the three of 'em are wanted for bank robbery in Wisconsin. A recent one. Anyway, he's more interested now in that angle of the case than in heckling Madge."

"Did you get Bassett drunk on purpose tonight?"

"A man's like a horse, Ed. You can lead him to whiskey but you can't make him drink. You didn't see me pouring any whiskey down him, did you?"

"No," I admitted. "I didn't see you grabbing it away, either."

"You got a nasty suspicious mind," he said. "But just the same, we got the morning free. He'll sleep till noon, and we'll be ahead of him with the insurance company."

"Why do you care about that—now that we got a lead on Reynolds?"

"Kid, we don't know *why* this Reynolds was interested in your dad. I got a hunch if we find out the inside story of why Wally carried that much insurance—and kept it secret that he was carrying it—we might get an idea. I'd just as soon have some idea what it's all about before we go up against Reynolds. Also we can't make a move till we get the listing on that phone number, so what have we got to lose but sleep?"

"The hell with sleep," I said.

"Okay. You're young; you'll live through it. *I* ought to have more sense, but I guess I haven't. Shall we get some more coffee?"

I looked at Thompson's clock. I said, "We got over an hour before the offices open downtown. I'll go get the coffee, and then you can tell me more about what you and Pop did when you were together."

The hour went pretty quick.

CHAPTER 10

THE CENTRAL MUTUAL turned out to be a moderate-sized branch office of a company whose headquarters were in St. Louis. It was a break for us; the smaller the office the more likely they were to remember Pop.

We asked for the manager and were taken into his office. Uncle Am did the talking and explained who we were.

The manager said, "No, I don't recall him offhand, but I'll have our records checked. You say the policy hasn't turned up yet. That won't matter, if it's on our records, and paid up." He smiled slightly, deprecatingly. "We're not a racket, you know. The policy is merely our client's record of a contract that exists and will be kept, whether or not his copy is lost or destroyed."

Uncle Am said, "I understand that. What we're interested in is whether you recall any circumstances about the policy—for instance, just why its existence was kept a secret from his family. He must have given a reason, some reason, to the agent who sold him the policy."

The manager said, "Just a minute." He went out into the general office and came back a few minutes later. He said, "The head clerk is looking up the file. He'll bring it in personally, and maybe he'll be able to recall the insured."

My uncle asked, "How unusual is it for a man to keep a policy secret that way?"

"It's not unique. It *is* highly unusual. The only other case I can recall offhand is that of a man who had a touch of persecution complex. He was afraid his relatives might do away with him if they knew he was insured. Yet, paradoxically, he loved them and wished to provide for them in case of his death. Uh—I didn't mean to imply that in this case—"

"Of course not," Uncle Am said.

A tall gray-haired man came into the office with a file folder in his hand. He said, "Here's the Wallace Hunter file, Mr. Bradbury. Yes, I recall him. Always came into the office to make his payments. There's a notation clipped to the file that no notices were to be sent out."

The manager took the file folder. He asked, "Ever talk to him, Henry? Ever ask him *why* the notices were not to be mailed, for instance?"

The tall man shook his head. "No, Mr. Bradbury."

"All right, Henry."

The tall man went out.

The manager was leafing through the file. He said, "Yes, it's paid up. There are two small loans against it—made to meet premium payments. They'll be deducted from the face of the policy, but they won't amount to much." He turned another couple of pages. He said, "Oh, the policy wasn't sold from this office. It was transferred here from Gary, Indiana."

"Would they have any records on it there?"

"No, aside from a duplicate of this file at the main office in St. Louis, there are no other records. This file was transferred here from Gary at the time Mr. Hunter moved to Chicago. I see by the dates that was just a few weeks after the policy was taken out."

Uncle Am asked, "Would the policy itself show any details not given in that file?"

"No, the policy is a standard straight-life form, with the name and amount and date filled in. Pasted inside it is a photostatic copy of the application for the policy—but the original of that photostat is here in this file. You may see that if you wish."

He handed Uncle Am the file, opened to a form filled in with pen and ink, and I walked over behind Uncle Am's chair so I could read it over his shoulder. I made a mental note of the date of the application, and the signature of the agent who sold it—Paul B. Anderz.

Uncle Am asked, "Do you know if this agent, Anderz, is still working out of your Gary office?"

"No, I don't. We can write them and find out."

Uncle Am said, "Never mind, thanks anyway. You'll want a copy of the death certificate, of course?"

"Yes, before we can issue a check to the beneficiary. This young man's mother, I take it."

"His stepmother." Uncle Am handed back the folder and stood up. "Thanks a lot. Oh, by the way—was the policy paid quarterly?"

The manager did some leafing through the folder again. He said, "Yes, after the first payment. He paid a year's premium in advance with the original application."

Uncle Am thanked him again, and we left.

"Gary?" I asked.

"Yeah. We can get there on the el, can't we?"

"Less than an hour, I think." I thought for a minute. "Gosh, less than an hour from the Loop, and yet I never went back there after we left."

"Did Wally or Madge ever go back? For a visit, or anything?"

I thought, and then shook my head. "Not that I remember. I don't believe any of us ever went back there. Of course, I was only thirteen when we came from there to Chicago, but I think I'd remember."

"Tell me—wait, let's wait till we're on the train."

He didn't say any more till we had a seat on the Gary Express. Then he said, "All right, kid, let go. Relax, and tell me everything you can remember about Gary."

I said, "I went to Twelfth Street School. So did Gardie. I was in the eighth grade and she was in the fourth. When we left, I mean. We lived in a little frame house on Holman Street, three blocks from the school. The school had a band, and I wanted to get in it. They lent instruments and I borrowed a trombone. I was getting so I could read simple stuff on it, but Mom hated it. She called it 'that damn horn,' and I had to go out in the woodshed to practice. Then when we came to Chicago we lived in a flat and I couldn't have practiced even if Mom had liked it, so I—"

"Forget the trombone," Uncle Am said. "Get back to Gary."

I said, "We had a car part of the time, and part of the time we didn't. Pop worked at two or three different printing shops at one time or another. He was out of work for a while with arthritis in his arms and we went way in debt. I don't think we ever quite got out. I have a hunch we left so suddenly because we were running out on some of the debts we still had."

"You left suddenly?"

"It seems to me we did. I mean, I don't remember it being talked over. All of a sudden the van was there loading our furniture, and Pop had a job in Chicago and we had to leave right— Wait a minute—"

"Take your time, kid. I think you're getting at something. My God, Ed, what a sap I've been."

"You? How?"

He laughed. "I've been overlooking my best witness because I was too close to see him. Forget it. Get back to Gary."

I said, "I remember now. Something that was funny at the time, but I'd clean forgotten until I started talking about moving. I didn't know we were moving to Chicago until we got here. Pop said we were moving to Joliet; that's about twenty-five miles from Gary, same as Chicago, but west instead of northwest, and I remember telling all my kid friends we were going to Joliet—and then it turned out to be Chicago. Pop said he'd got a good job in Chicago and changed his mind about taking the one in Joliet. I remember, it seemed kind of funny to me, even then."

Uncle Am had his eyes closed. He said, "Go on, kid. Dig as deep as you can. You're doing swell."

"After we got to Chicago, we moved in right where we're still living. But Pop couldn't have been telling the truth about the job in Chicago, because he was around home the first few weeks after we came to Chi. Not all the time; but enough so I know he wasn't working. Then he got the job at Elwood Press."

"Back to Gary, kid. You keep ending up in Chicago."

"Well, we did," I said. "What do you want? The time Gardie had the mumps, or what?"

"I guess we can do without that. But keep on trying. Dig way down."

I said, "I remember vaguely something about a court. I can't remember what."

"Some creditor get a judgment against you?"

"That could be. I don't remember. I don't think Pop was

working the last week or two we were in Gary. But I don't remember whether he'd lost a job or been laid off, or what. Say,
that was the week he took all of us to the circus."

Uncle Am nodded. "And you sat in the reserved seats."

"Yeah, we—What made you say that?"

"Don't you see what you've been telling me, kid? Take what
we learned at the insurance company this morning and use it as
one piece of a jigsaw, use the little things you've been giving me
as other pieces, and what do you get?"

I said, "We lammed out of Gary. We moved suddenly and
without telling anybody where we were going. We even left a
false trail. But it was just because we owed so much, wasn't it?"

"Kid, I'll bet you a buck. You figure out what stores you dealt
with while you were there. You'll remember the grocery, anyway. Go round today and ask 'em—I'll bet you a buck Wally
paid off everything he owed in cash before you left."

"How could he, if he was out of work? Hell, we were broke
most of the time. And— Oh-oh."

"You begin to see it, Ed?"

"The insurance policy," I said. "It was about that time he
took it out. And he paid a year's premium in cash, in advance.
On five thousand, that'd run over a hundred bucks. And he'd
have needed cash to pay for getting moved to Chicago, and paying rent on the new place."

"And," said Uncle Am, "living a few weeks without working
in Gary and a few weeks before he started working in Chicago.
And taking the whole kaboodle of you to the circus. Now that
you're on the track, what can you add?"

I said, "Gardie and I got some new clothes to start school in
Chicago. You'd win the buck, Uncle Am. He had a windfall,
and it must have been at least three weeks before we left Gary.

And if you're right that he'd have paid off debts out of it, it must have been—ummm—at least five hundred bucks, maybe even a thousand."

Uncle Am said, "I'll settle for it being a thousand. Wally'd have paid off those debts. He was funny that way. Well, kid, here comes Gary. We'll see what we can find out."

We went for a phone book right at the station, and first we looked up the office of the Central Mutual. Uncle Am went into the phone booth to call them.

He came out looking disappointed. He said, "Anderz isn't with 'em any more. He quit about three years ago. Last they'd heard of him he was in Springfield, Illinois."

I said, "That's pretty far—a hundred and fifty miles. But look, maybe he's got a phone in his own name. It's an unusual enough name; we could try."

Uncle Am said, "I don't think we'll even bother, kid. The more I think of it, the less I think of it. I mean, Wally wouldn't have told him anything. He wouldn't have told him where his windfall came from. He'd have had to give him some reason for not wanting the premium notices mailed to him, but I'll bet ten, five and even that it wouldn't be the real reason. I think we've got a better lead."

"Who?"

"You, Ed. I want you to do some more thinking. Do you remember how to get out to where you used to live?"

I nodded. "East End car; you catch it a block from here."

We rode out and I remembered the corner where we got off. Hardly a thing had changed. The same drugstore was on the corner there, and in the block and a half we had to walk from the car, hardly a building had changed.

The house was across the street. It was smaller than I remembered, and it was badly in need of paint. It couldn't have been painted since we'd lived there.

I said, "The fence is different. We used to have a higher one."

Uncle Am chuckled. He said, "Look at it again, kid."

I did, and it was an old fence all right. It made me feel funny to realize that I remembered that fence as being chest-high. It wasn't the fence that had changed; it was me.

We crossed the street.

I put my hand on the fence, and a big police dog came running out from the side of the house. It wasn't barking; it meant business. I pulled my hand back, and the dog didn't jump the fence. It stopped, growling.

I said, "Looks like I'm not welcome there any more."

We walked on past, slowly, the dog keeping pace with us inside the fence. I kept looking at the house. It was pretty much of a mess; the porch was sagging and the wooden steps were crooked and one of them was broken. The yard was littered with junk.

We kept on walking. The grocery down on the corner still had the same name on the window. I said, "Let's go in."

The man who came to wait on us looked familiar, but I got that funny feeling again. He was a little man; he should have been a big one. Outside of that, I recognized him, all right.

I asked for cigarettes and then said, "Remember me, Mr. Hagendorf? I used to live down the block."

He looked at me closely. After a few seconds he said, "Not the Hunter boy, are you?"

"Yep," I said. "Ed Hunter."

He said, "I'll be damned." He put out his hand. "You moving back in the neighborhood?"

"No," I told him. "But my uncle's moving near here. This is

my uncle, Mr. Hagendorf, Ambrose Hunter. He's going to live near here. I thought I'd bring him in and introduce him to you."

Uncle Am shook hands with the grocer and said, "Yeah, Ed told me I ought to deal here. Thought I might open an account."

Hagendorf said, "We don't do much credit business, but I guess it's all right." He grinned at me. He said, "Your dad sure got me in the red sometimes, but he paid it off before he left."

I said, "It was a pretty big bill, wasn't it?"

"High as it had ever been. Something over a hundred bucks; I forget exactly. But he paid it off, all right. How are things going in Joliet, Ed?"

"Pretty good," I told him. "Well, we'll be seeing you, Mr. Hagendorf."

We went out and I said, "You sure pick 'em, Uncle Am. Are you the seventh son of a seventh son? And thanks for being quick on the uptake in there. I thought if we could find out without coming right out and asking—"

"Sure. Well, kid—?"

I said, "You go on over to the car line. Wait for me by the drugstore."

Alone, I walked a couple of times around the block. I kept across the street from our house when I went by, so the dog wouldn't distract me by keeping pace along the fence. I stopped and leaned against a tree where I could watch the house, and see the windows of the upper front room where I'd slept, the windows of the dining room.

I wanted to cry, a little bit, but I swallowed the lump in my throat and let myself go back and remember things. I tried to keep my mind on the last month we'd been there.

One of those last weeks, it came to me, Pop hadn't been working, exactly. Yet he'd been gone. For a few days he'd been gone day and night, doing something. Not out of town, or was it? No.

I had it, and wondered why I hadn't remembered before. Maybe because, for some reason, it had never been talked about afterwards. It seemed to me that Pop had gone out of his way not to mention it again, now that I remembered.

I went over to where Uncle Am was waiting under the awning of the drugstore. There was a streetcar coming. I just nodded to him and we caught the car.

As we rode back downtown I told him. "Jury duty. Pop was on a jury a little while before we left."

"What kind of a case, kid?"

"I don't know. He never talked about it. We can look up in the files at a newspaper and see what was going on then. I guess that's why I forgot it; we never talked about it."

He looked at his watch. "We'll get downtown about noon. You can phone this Bunny Wilson about the listing first."

We got a lot of change so I could keep dropping coins if I had to; and I called Bunny. I made the call from a quiet hotel lobby and left the booth door open so Uncle Am could hear.

Bunny said, "I got it for you, Ed. It's in the name of Raymond, Apartment Forty-three, Milan Towers. That's an apartment hotel on Ontario Street over between Michigan Boulevard and the Lake."

I said, "I think I know where it is. Thanks to hell and back, Bunny."

"Don't mention it, Ed. I wish I could help you more. If there's anything I can do, at all, let me know. I'll even take a night off work, any time you say. How you coming? Say, when Mrs. Horth called me just now she said it was long distance. Where you calling from?"

"Gary," I told him. "We came here to see a guy named Anderz who sold Pop that insurance policy."

"What policy, Ed?"

I forgot I hadn't told him about it. I told him, and he said, "I'll be damned, Ed. Well, that's good news for Madge. I was worried how she'd get along. That'll help out plenty, getting her started on her own. Did you see the guy you mentioned?"

"No, Anderz moved to Springfield. We aren't going to follow him. Probably wouldn't find out anything anyway. We're coming back. Well, thanks again and so long."

At the *Gary Times* office we got them to show us the back volume covering the date we were looking for.

It wasn't any hunt at all. It was on the front page. That was the week of the trial of Steve Reynolds for bank robbery. The trial had lasted three days and had ended in a verdict of guilty. He'd drawn life. One Harry Reynolds, his brother, had been a witness for the defense and had tried to alibi him. Obviously the alibi had not been believed, but for some reason not appearing in the newspapers there hadn't been any prosecution for perjury.

The defense attorney had been Schweinberg, a notorious mouthpiece for crooks who, I recalled, had been disbarred about a year ago.

There were photographs with the day-by-day accounts of the trial. One of Steve Reynolds. One of Harry. I studied them until I was sure I'd know them, especially Harry.

We finished and gave back the bound volume. We thanked them and left.

Uncle Am said, "I think we can go back to Chicago now, Ed. We don't know the details, but we got enough. We can guess most of the rest."

I asked, "What can't we guess?"

"Why he could wait three weeks after the trial before he lammed. Look, here's how I read it. Wally gets put on the Reynolds jury. This Schweinberg was disbarred for bribing jurors; that was his racket. Somehow he got to Wally and gave him a thousand bucks, more or less, to vote acquittal. He couldn't have hoped for anything more than to split the jury and get a mistrial, from the evidence.

"Wally took it—and crossed him up. Wally had nerve, all right; he might have done that. Hell, he must have. He got about a thousand from somewhere. Right after the trial he uses part of it for an insurance policy—one big enough to carry Madge till you kids were through school. Then he lammed out of Gary and covered his trail so they couldn't find him. I don't know why he waited three weeks; there must have been something protected him for that long. Maybe they did hold Harry Reynolds for a while, intending him to get a stretch for perjury or as an accessory, then let him go. And with Harry loose, Wally would know he'd be gunned for."

I asked, "Do you suppose Mom knew about it?"

He shrugged his shoulders. "She must have known part of it. My guess is she didn't know much. We know he didn't tell her about the insurance policy he took out. Maybe she didn't know any of it. He could have told her he hit on a policy ticket to account for having extra dough. Maybe he let her think you were ducking Gary to run out on those old bills—he could have paid them without her knowing it."

I said, "It doesn't make sense, does it? He's honest enough to pay bills he *could* have run out on, since he was running anyway, but still he takes money from gangsters for a bribe—"

"Ah, that's the difference, kid. The way Wally'd figure it, it isn't dishonest to cheat a crook. Hell, I don't know if he was right or wrong about that; I don't care. It took plenty of guts to take dough for a thing like that and *not* deliver."

We didn't talk much, riding back to Chicago.

In the Loop, we transferred to a Howard Express and got off at Grand. I said, "I better go home and take a bath and put on clean clothes. I feel sticky."

Uncle Am nodded. He said, "Look, kid, we can't keep on forever without sleeping, either. You do that and take a nap, too. It's about two o'clock. Get a little sleep and come to the hotel around seven or eight. We'll take a look at the Milan Towers this evening, but we don't want to be dopey when we do it."

At our place, I went on upstairs and Uncle Am kept on over toward the Wacker.

The door was locked and I had to let myself in with my key. I was just as glad nobody was home. I had a bath and was in bed within twenty minutes. I set my alarm for seven.

When it went off and woke me up, there were voices in the living room. I put on the rest of my clothes and went out there. Mom and Gardie were home and Bunny was with them. They had just finished eating, and Mom said, "Hello, stranger," and wanted to know if I wanted to eat. I said I'd just get myself a cup and have coffee.

I got a cup and pulled up a chair. I couldn't get over looking at Mom. She'd been to a beauty parlor, and she sure looked different. She had on a black dress, a new one, but it made her look better than I'd ever seen her. She had on a little make-up, but not too much.

Gosh, I thought, she's really pretty when she's fixed up.

Gardie looked pretty good, too. But her face got a little sullen when she looked at me. I had a hunch she was holding it against me about the wallet business, and my little scrap with Bobby Reinhart.

Bunny said, "They're talking about going to Florida, Ed, as soon as they get the insurance money. I tell 'em they ought to stay here, where they got friends."

"Friends, nuts," Mom said. "Who outside of you, Bunny? Ed, I hear you were in Gary this morning. Did you see the old place?"

I nodded. "Just from the outside."

Mom said, "It sure was a dump. This flat's bad enough, but it sure was a dump, in Gary."

I didn't say anything.

I put sugar and cream in the coffee Mom poured for me. It wasn't very hot so I drank it right down. I said, "I got to meet Uncle Am. I can't stay."

Bunny said, "Gee, Ed, we were counting on you to play some cards. When we found you were home, Madge looked at your clock and found you were going to wake up at seven. We thought you'd stick around."

I said, "Maybe I can bring Uncle Am back with me. I'll see."

I stood up. Gardie asked, "What are you going to do, Eddie? I don't mean now, I mean in general. You going back to work?"

"Sure," I said, "I'm going back to work. Why not?"

"I thought maybe you'd want to come to Florida with us, that's all. You don't, do you?"

I said, "I guess not."

She said, "The money's Mom's. I don't know if you know, but the policy was made out to her. It's hers."

Mom said, "Gardie!"

"I know that," I said. "I don't want any of the money."

Mom said, "Gardie shouldn't of put it that way, Ed. But

what she means is you've got a job and everything, and I've got to finish putting her through school and—"

"It's all right, Mom," I told her. "Honest, I never even thought about wanting any of the money. I'm doing all right. Well, so long. So long, Bunny."

Bunny called out, "Wait a second, Ed," and joined me in the hall by the door. He pulled out a five-dollar bill. He said, "Bring your uncle over, Ed; I'd like to meet him. And bring some beer back with you. Out of this."

I didn't take the bill. I said, "Honest, Bunny, I can't. I'd like you to meet him, but some other time. We got something to do this evening. We're—well, you know what we're trying to do."

He shook his head slowly. He said, "There's no percentage in it, Ed. You ought to let it lay."

"Maybe," I said. "Maybe you're right, Bunny. But now we're started; well, we're going to see it through. It's goofy I guess, but that's the way it is."

"Then how about letting me help?"

"You did. You helped plenty, getting that listing for us. If anything else comes up, I'll let you know. Thanks a lot, Bunny."

At the hotel, I found Uncle Am shaving with an electric razor plugged in beside his bureau mirror.

He asked, "Get sleep?"

"Sure, lots of it." I took a look at his face in the mirror. It was a little puffy and his eyes were slightly red-rimmed. I said, "You didn't, did you?"

"I started to, and Bassett came around and woke me up. We took each other around for a drink and pumped each other."

"Dry?" I asked.

"I don't know how dry I got him—I think he's holding something back, but I don't know what. In fact, I wouldn't be surprised, Ed, if he's running a ring-tailed whizzer on us. But I can't figure where."

"And how did he do with you?"

"Not so bad. I told him about Gary, about the trial, about the extra dough Wally had—I gave him everything but the Milan Towers address and phone number. I got a hunch he's holding back something more important than that."

"As for instance?"

"I wish I knew, kid. Have you seen Madge?"

"She's going to Florida," I told him. "She and Gardie. Soon as they get the insurance."

He said, "I wish 'em luck. She'll land on her feet, kid. That money won't last her over a year, but she'll have another husband by then. She's still got her figure and—she was about six or seven years younger than Wally, if I remember right."

"She's thirty-six, I think."

Uncle Am said, "Bassett and I had a drink or two and then I got rid of him and there wasn't enough time left to sleep before you'd get here, so I went over and cased the Milan Towers. I made a start for us."

He came over and sat on the bed, leaned back against the pillow. He said, "There's a girl living alone in Apartment Forty-three. Name of Claire Raymond. Tasty dish, the bartender says. Her husband's away; the bartender thinks they're separated. He even thinks she got walked out on; but the rent's paid till the end of the month so she's staying there alone for that long, anyway."

"Did you find out if—"

"Yeah, Raymond is Reynolds. He fits the description, anyway. And he'd been in the bar with a couple of friends that could be Dutch and Benny."

"Benny?"

"The wop torpedo. I got his name from Bassett; Bassett had looked up what the cops had on them, and gave me some dope. Benny Rosso. Dutch's last name is Reagan, if you can figure that out. None of them has shown at the Milan for about a week—that'd be from a day or two before Wally's death."

"Figure that means anything?"

He yawned. "I wouldn't know. We'll have to ask 'em sometime. Well, I guess we might as well get going."

I said, "Relax a minute. I got to go down the hall."

"Okay, kid. Don't fall in."

I went down the hall, and when I came back he was sound asleep.

I stood there a minute, thinking. He'd been doing ninetenths of this by himself, with me playing tagalong. Didn't I have the brains or nerve to do something by myself for once? Especially when he needed sleep and I didn't.

I took a deep breath and let it out and said to myself, "Here goes nothing," and I turned out the light.

I got out without waking him up, and I headed for the Milan Towers.

CHAPTER 11

I SLOWED DOWN on the way, because it came to me I didn't know what I was going to do. It was pretty early in the evening, too, and I was hungry, so I stopped and ate. When I was through eating, I still didn't have any idea.

But I went on to the Milan Towers.

There was a cocktail bar in the corner of the building, connecting with the lobby. I went in and sat down at the bar. It was swanky as hell. I'd been going to order beer, but I'd have felt foolish ordering beer in a place like that.

I tilted my hat back a little and tried to feel tough.

"Rye," I told the bartender. I remembered George Raft, as Ned Beaumont in the movie, *The Glass Key,* always ordered rye. I tried to feel like George Raft had acted.

The bartender spun a shot glass expertly along the bar and filled it from an Old Overholt bottle. "Wash?"

"Plain water," I told him.

I got back thirty-five cents out of the dollar bill I put on the bar.

I thought, I don't have to be in any hurry to drink it. Without turning around, I studied the place, using the mirror back of the bar. I wondered, why do all bars have mirrors? I should think when a man's getting tight, the last thing he'd want to watch would be himself in a mirror. At least the ones who drink to get away from themselves.

In the mirror I could see through the door that led into the lobby of the hotel. I could see a clock in there. The dial of the clock was backwards in the mirror and it took me a little while to figure out that it was a quarter after nine.

At half-past nine, I thought, I'll do something. I don't know what, but I'll get started.

The first step will be to go out in the lobby and phone upstairs. But what am I going to say?

I wished now I'd either waked Uncle Am or waited for him. Maybe I was going to make a botch of things. Like I did taking a poke at Reinhart.

I looked around the place again, in the mirror. Down at the other end of the bar a man sat alone. He looked like a successful business man. I thought, I wonder if he is. For all I know, he might be a gangster. And the little, dark, Italian fellow sitting alone over in the booth, might be a commission merchant, although he looked like a torpedo. He might even be Benny Rosso. I could ask him, but if he is, he's heeled and I'm not. And maybe he wouldn't tell me.

I took a sip of the rye and it tasted lousy, so I drank it down to get rid of it, and got hold of the chaser before I desecrated that sleek and shiny bar by exploding across it. I hoped nobody had noticed my lack of dignity in that dive for the water.

I looked at the backwards clock in the mirror and it looked like three thirty-one, so I figured out it was nine twenty-nine.

The bartender was coming back my way, but I shook my head at him. I wondered if he'd seen me almost choke on the drink. I felt silly, but I sat there one more minute and then I got up and started for the lobby door. I felt like my shirttail was hanging out and everybody was looking at it.

I was going to stutter into the phone and mess everything.

It was the juke box that saved me. It was between the bar and that door, against a square pillar in the middle of the room. It was bright and shiny and gaudy, even in that swanky barroom. I stopped to look over the numbers on it and fished a nickel out of my pocket.

I picked a Benny Goodman out of the lot and dropped my nickel. I stood there watching the machine slide the platter out of the stack and bring down the needle.

I closed my eyes when it started to play and stood there taking in the introduction, not moving a muscle, but giving to the music with all of my body, with all of me, letting go inside.

Then I opened my eyes again and walked out into the lobby, riding on the high wail of the clarinet, drunk as a lord. Not from the rye.

I felt swell. I didn't feel like a kid, I didn't feel foolish, and my shirttail was in again. I could handle anything likely to happen and most things that were unlikely.

I stepped into the phone booth and dialed W-E-N-3-8-4-2. I heard the buzz of the phone ringing.

The click of the receiver and a girl's voice said, "Hello?" The voice I'd liked last night.

I said, "This is Ed, Claire."

"Ed who?"

"You don't know me. You've never met me. But I'm calling from the lobby downstairs. Are you alone?"

"Y-yes. Who *is* this?"

I asked, "Does the name Hunter mean anything to you?"

"Hunter? It doesn't."

I asked, "How about the name Reynolds?"

"Who *is* this?"

"I'd like to explain," I said. "May I come upstairs? Or would you meet me down in the bar for a drink?"

"Are you a friend of Harry's?"

"No."

"I don't know you," she said. "I don't see why I should see you."

I said, "That's the only way you'll get to know me."

"Do you *know* Harry?"

I said, "I'm an enemy of Harry's."

"Oh." It stalled her for a minute.

I said, "I'm coming upstairs. Open the door but leave the chain on it. If I don't look like a werewolf—or any other kind of wolf—maybe you'll unhook the chain."

I hung up before she could tell me not to. I thought I had her curious, enough so to let me in.

I didn't want to give her time to think it over, nor time to make a phone call. I didn't wait for an elevator; I hotfooted it up three flights of stairs.

She hadn't phoned anybody, because she was waiting at the door. There was a chain on it, all right, and she had the door open four inches on the chain and was standing there looking out. That way she could see me walking down the hall and get a better look than by opening it after I knocked.

She was young, and she was a knockout. Even through four inches of open door, I could see that. She was the kind of girl that could make you whistle twice.

I managed to get down the hall without stumbling on the carpet.

Her eyes stayed neutral, but she took the chain off the door when I got there. She opened it, and I went in. There wasn't anyone waiting back of the door with a sandbag, so I went on into the living room. It was a nice room except that it was a little like a movie set. There was a fireplace with brass andirons and a stand that held a dainty, shiny poker and shovel, but there'd never been a fire in the fireplace. There was a comfortable looking sofa in front of it. There were lamps and drapes and curtains and things; I can't describe it, but it was a nice room.

I walked around to the front of the sofa and sat down. I held my hands out to the empty fireplace and rubbed them as though I were warming them.

I said, "It's a braw night. The snow is seven feet deep on the boulevard. My huskies gave out before I reached Ontario. The last mile I had to crawl on hand and knee." I rubbed my hands some more.

She stood there at the end of the sofa, looking down at me, arms akimbo. They were nice arms for a sleeveless dress, and she was wearing a sleeveless dress.

She said, "I take it you're not in a hurry?"

I said, "I must catch a train a week from Wednesday."

She made a little noise that might have been a well-bred snort. She said, "I suppose we might as well have a drink then."

She bent down and opened the cabinet to the left of the fireplace and there was a row of bottles in it and a row of glasses. There were jiggers and stirring spoons and a shaker and—as God is my witness—there was a miniature freezing compartment at one side with three rubber trays of ice cubes.

I said, "What, no radio in it?"

"The other side of the fireplace. Radio-phono." I looked that way.

I said, "I'll bet you haven't any records."

"Do you want a drink, or don't you?"

I looked back at the row of bottles, and decided against anything mixed; I might be expected to mix it myself and not know how to. I said, "Burgundy goes well with a maroon carpet. It doesn't make spots if you spill it."

"If that's all that worries you, you can have crème de menthe. The furnishings aren't mine."

"But you have to live with them."

"Not after next week."

I said, "Then to hell with Burgundy. We'll have crème de menthe. Anyway me, I will."

She took a pair of tiny liqueur goblets from the top shelf and filled them from the crème de menthe bottle. She handed me one.

I saw a teakwood cigarette box on the mantel. I gave her one of her own cigarettes and lighted it for her, lighted one for myself and then sat down and took a sip of the liqueur. It tasted like peppermint candy and looked like green ink. I decided that I liked it.

She didn't sit down. She stood leaning back against the mantel, looking at me.

She was still neutral.

She had jet-black hair that managed to be sleek and wavy at the same time. She was slender, almost as tall as I. She had clear, calm eyes.

I said, "You're beautiful."

A corner of her mouth twitched a little bit. She asked, "Is that why you telephoned up, to tell me that?"

I said, "I didn't know it then. I'd never seen you. No, that wasn't why I wanted to talk to you."

"What do I have to do to get you started talking?"

"Liquor always helps," I said. "And I'm a sucker for music. *Do* you have any records?"

She took a deep drag on her cigarette and let the smoke out her nostrils, slowly. She said, "If I asked you how you got that black eye, I suppose you'd tell me you were bitten by a St. Bernard."

I said, "Nothing but the truth. A man hit me."

"Why?"

"He didn't like me."

"Did you hit him back?"

I said, "Yes."

She laughed. It was a full, honest laugh. She said, "I don't know whether you're crazy or not. I can't decide. What do you really want?"

I said, "Harry Reynold's address."

She frowned. "I don't have it. I don't know where he is. I don't care."

I said, "We were talking about phonograph records. Do you have—"

"Stop it. I want to know; why are you looking for Harry?"

I took a long breath and leaned forward. I said, "Last week a man was killed in an alley. He was my father, a printer. I'm an apprentice printer. I'm not as old as I look. My uncle is a carney. He and I are trying to find Harry Reynolds to turn him over to the police for killing my father. My uncle would be here with me, but he's asleep. He's a swell guy; you'd like him."

She said, "You do better in monosyllables. You were telling the truth about that black eye."

I said, "Then shall we try monosyllables again?"

She took another sip of the liqueur, watching me over the rim of the tiny glass.

"All right," she said. "What's your name?"

"Ed."

"Is that all of it? What's the rest?"

"Hunter," I told her. "That took two syllables. I tried to stick to Ed; it's all your fault."

"You really *are* looking for Harry? That's why you came here?"

"Yes."

"What do you want with him?"

"That'll take three syllables."

"Go ahead."

"To kill him."

"Who are you working for?"

"A man. His name wouldn't mean anything to you. If I thought it would, I'd tell you."

She said, "Your tongue isn't quite loose enough yet. We'll have to try more liquor." She refilled our glasses.

"And music," I told her, "soothes the savage breast. How about those records. If you have any."

She laughed again, and walked across the room. She pulled aside some cretonne and there was a shelf of albums. "Who do you want, Ed? Most of them are here."

"Dorsey?"

"Both of them. Which Dorsey?"

"The trombone Dorsey."

She knew I meant Tommy. She took the records from one of the albums and put them in the phono, setting it for automatic.

She came back and stood in front of me. "Who sent you here?"

I said, "It would be a nice line if I could say 'Benny sent me.'

But he didn't. I don't like Benny or Dutch any more than I like Harry. Nobody sent me, Claire. I just came."

She leaned over and touched both sides of my coat, where a shoulder holster would be. She straightened up, frowning. She said, "You haven't even got a—"

"Shut up," I said, "I want to hear Dorsey."

She shrugged, picked up her glass from the mantel and sat down on the sofa, just far enough away to let me know I wasn't expected to make a pass. I didn't. I wanted to, but I didn't.

I waited till the phonograph finished the fourth record and quit.

Then I said, "What if there was money in it for you? For Harry's address, I mean."

She said, "I don't know it, Ed."

She turned and looked at me. She said, "Listen, this is the truth and I don't care if you believe it or not. I'm through with Harry and with—with everything he stands for. I've lived here two years now, and all I've got to show for it is enough money to get back home on. Home is Indianapolis.

"I'm getting out of here and going back there, and I'm going to take a job and live in a hall bedroom, with one pillow on the bed. I can learn all over again how to live on twenty-five bucks a week. Or whatever. Maybe that sounds funny to you."

"Not particularly," I said. "But wouldn't a nest egg in the bank be a good start for turning over a new—"

"No, Ed. For two perfectly good reasons. First, a double-cross would be a hell of a start. Second, I don't know where Harry is. I haven't seen him for a week—almost two weeks. I don't even know if he's in Chicago. I don't care."

I said, "If that's the way it is—"

I got up and walked over to the shelf of albums. There was a book of old-timers there, featuring Jimmy Noone. Wang-Wang Blues, Wabash Blues—I'd heard a lot about Jimmy Noone, and I'd never heard one of his platters. I took the album over to the phono, figured out how to put it on, and stood watching till the first record got going. It was very, very swell stuff.

I held out my hand to Claire, and she stood up and came to me. We danced. The music was as blue as the crème de menthe had been green. Deep, deep blue. They don't play it like that any more. It got me.

It wasn't until the music stopped that I really realized I had Claire in my arms. And that she wasn't fighting to get out of them and that kissing her was going to be the most natural thing in the world.

It was. And it was there, in the silence between records, in the silence of that kiss, that we heard a key turning in the door.

She was out of my arms almost before I realized what the sound was.

She put a finger to her lips in a quick gesture of silence and then pointed toward a door that was ajar just to the left of the liquor cabinet. Then she whirled and started for the short hallway that led to the outer door of the apartment—the door in which the key had turned, the door that was opening by now.

I wasn't so slow, either. I got my glass and my cigarette off the mantel and my hat off the end of the sofa, and I was through the door she'd pointed to, all before she'd reached the doorway to the hall.

I was in a dark room. I pushed the door back as it had been, a few inches ajar.

I heard her voice say, "Dutch! What the hell do you mean by walking in here like—"

The phono started in again, on the second of the Jimmy

Noone records, and I couldn't hear the rest. The record was Margie. "Margie, I'm always thinking of you, Margie—"

Through the crack of the door, I could see Claire crossing the room to shut it off. Her face was white with anger and her eyes—well, I'm glad they hadn't looked at me like that.

She shut it off, sharp. She said, "Goddam you, Dutch, did Harry give you that key or did you—"

"Now, Claire, climb off it. No, Harry didn't give me a key. You know damn well he wouldn't. *I* got this key, toots. I figured this angle a week ago."

"What angle? Skip it; I don't even want to know what you're talking about. Get out of here."

"Now, toots." He was farther into the room now. I saw him for the first time. I hadn't been able to tell anything by his voice except that he wasn't a soprano. I saw him now. He looked as big as the side of the house.

And if he was either Dutch or Irish, then I was a Hottentot. He looked like a Greek to me. A Greek or a Syrian or an Armenian. Maybe even Turkish or Persian or something. But how he got the last name of Reagan or the nickname Dutch, I wouldn't try to guess. He had swarthy skin, and if he'd been stripped, there would have been acres of it. He looked like a wrestler and walked as though he were muscle-bound.

"Now, toots," he said, "don't get up in the air like that. Take it easy. We got business to talk."

"Get *out* of here."

He stood there, smiling, turning his hat in his hands. His voice got softer.

He said, "You think I don't know Harry's crossing me? Me and Benny? Well, I'm not worried about Benny, but me, I don't like to be crossed. I'm going to explain that to Harry."

"I don't know what you're talking about."

"Don't you?" He took a fat cigar out of his breast pocket, put it between his puffy lips, and took his time lighting it with a silver lighter. He put his hat back on his head. He said again, "Don't you?"

Claire said, "I don't. And if you don't get out of here, I'll—"

"You'll what?" He chuckled. "You'll call copper? With forty G's, hot from Waupaca, in the joint? Don't make me laugh. Now listen careful, toots. First, I know the score. Harry pretended to break with you; he was smart, he did it *before* the Waupaca job. But like schlemiels, we let Harry take the stuff when we break up. Now where's Harry? I don't know, but I'll find out. And I know where the forty G's are. Here."

"You're crazy. You damn dumb—"

I'd been wrong in thinking he was muscle-bound. He just walked that way. His hand went out like a snake would strike and grabbed Claire's wrist. He jerked her to him and her back was against him, his arm holding her there, against his chest, pinning down both her arms.

His other hand clamped over her mouth.

His back was mostly toward me. I didn't know what I was going to do; I didn't know what I could do against a mountain of muscle like that, but I opened the door. I looked around for something. The only thing I could see was the lightweight poker by the phony fireplace.

I started for it, walking quietly.

His voice hadn't changed a semitone in pitch. He kept on as though he was talking about the weather. He said, "Just a second, toots, I'll relax my hand over your yap enough to let you tell me yeah or no. One way we take the dough, you and me, toots, and Harry doesn't live here any more. Other way, well—you wouldn't like it."

I had hold of the poker now. My feet hadn't made any noise. Only, my God, it was a toy poker. It wasn't made to poke a fire or to hit a giant over the head with. It didn't have any heft. It would just make him mad.

The andirons were screwed down.

I remembered something I'd read. There's a jujitsu blow along the side of the neck, parallel to and just under the jawbone. It's given with the edge of the flat hand, and it can paralyze or even be fatal.

It was worth a try. I moved to just the right position, held the poker well back for a good swing.

I said, "Hold it, Dutch."

Plenty happened. He let go Claire with both hands, and turned his head at just the angle I'd figured he'd turn it, and I let go with the poker, a full arm swing. It hit on the dotted line that would have been there if his neck had been on a diagram.

Claire fell, and Dutch fell, and the double thud shook the Milan Towers. It really was a jar. It knocked Claire's crème de menthe glass off the mantel and it hit the tiles of the fireplace with a bright tinkle and a green splash. There were going to be spots on the maroon carpet after all.

My first thought was his gun. I didn't know if he was really out or for how long. It wasn't in a holster. It was a snub-nosed Police Positive revolver, in his side coat pocket.

Once I had it, I felt better. I could even hear what was going on, and what was going on was laughter. Claire was on her hands and knees trying to get up, and she was laughing like the devil. Slightly drunken laughter.

I didn't get it; she hadn't been drunk. It didn't sound like hysteria.

It wasn't. When she saw me looking at her, she stopped. She said, "Turn on the phonograph again, *quick.*"

Then she started laughing again. Only it was just her mouth that was laughing. Her face was white; her eyes were scared. She got to her feet and staggered across the room, deliberately.

I didn't get it, I was dumb. But I can take orders; I got the phonograph going. She collapsed onto the sofa, sobbing, but sobbing quietly, very quietly.

The phonograph played, "Margie, I'm always thinking of you, Margie; you mean the world—"

Over it, she said, "Talk, Ed. Talk loudly. *Walk,* so they can hear you." She'd stopped sobbing, and brought her voice up in pitch. "Don't you *see,* you dope? A fall like that, a noise like that? It's either a murder or an accident—or a drunk falling down. If there's talking and walking and laughing after it, then they say, it was just a drunk. If there's dead quiet after a thud like that, they call the desk—"

"Sure," I said. I'd whispered it. I cleared my throat and said, "Sure," louder. Too loud. I didn't try it a third time.

I still had the gun in my hand. I shoved it in my pocket to get it out of the way, and went over to where Dutch still lay stretched out. I thought, My God, why is he still as that? He can't be dead from—

But he was. My hand inside his coat couldn't find any heartbeat, although I kept hunting. I didn't believe it. A trick blow like that, you read it in a book, but you don't really believe it would work. Not for you. For a jujitsu expert, yes, but not for you.

I'd been so scared that it wouldn't even faze him that I'd put my weight into it. It had worked. He was as dead as a mackerel.

I started laughing, and not to reassure the neighbors.

Claire came over and slapped my face and I stopped.

We went back to the sofa and sat down. I got hold of myself, and got cigarettes out for us. I got hold of myself, and when I struck a match and held it for us, my hand was steady.

She asked, "Want a drink, Ed?"

"No," I told her.

She said, "Neither do I."

The phonograph had changed records again. It started the Wang-Wang Blues. I got up and shut it off. If the neighbors under us or on either side were going to call copper or call the desk, they'd have done it by now.

I sat back down on the sofa. Claire put her hand in mine, and we sat there, not looking at each other, not talking, staring into a fireplace that didn't have a fire in it and never would have.

Anyway, looking at the fireplace, we didn't have to look at Dutch on the floor behind us.

But he was there. He didn't get up and leave. He never would. He wouldn't ever do anything. He was dead.

And his being there got bigger and bigger until it filled the room.

Claire's hand tightened convulsively in mine and she started sobbing again, very quietly.

CHAPTER 12

I WAITED TILL SHE'D STOPPED CRYING and then I said, "We've got to do something. We can call the police and tell them the truth; that's one thing. Another; we can scram out of here and let them find it whenever they do. The third would be tougher; we could put it somewhere else for them to find."

"We *can't* call the police, Ed. They'd find out Harry had been living here. They'd find out everything. They'd nail me as an accessory to every job he ever pulled. They'd   " Her face got white as a sheet. "Ed, they *did* take me along on one job, made me wait in the car and act as lookout. God, what a sap I was not to see he was deliberately fixing me up so I could never talk. The police know Dutch was on that job, and if—"

I said, "Could they identify you, and tie you in with that job?"

"I—I think they could."

I said, "Then we'd better not call them. But you're getting out of here anyway, going back to Indianapolis. Couldn't you just leave tonight?"

"Yes, but—I'd be *wanted*. They could trace me when they found Dutch dead here. They could find out who I was and where I came from. I couldn't go back to Indianapolis; I'd have to go somewhere else. There'd be dodgers out for me. All the rest of my life, I'd be—"

I cut her short. "Okay," I said. "We can't call copper and we can't walk off and leave him. How could we get him out of here?"

"He's awful heavy, Ed. I don't know if we could do it, but there's a service elevator at the back of the hall that goes to a back door off the alley. And it's after midnight. But we'd need a car once we got him to the alley. And he's awful heavy, Ed. Do you think we could?"

I stood up and looked around till I saw the phone. I said, "I'll see what I can do, Claire. Wait."

I went over to the phone and called the Wacker, and I gave Uncle Am's room number.

When his voice answered, I felt so relieved my knees got weak and I sat down in the chair by the phone table.

I said, "This is Ed, Uncle Am."

"You young squirt, what you mean walking off on me? I been waiting for you to call. I suppose you got yourself in a jam, huh?"

I said, "I suppose I did. I'm calling from—from the phone number we had."

"The hell. You're doing all right, kid. Or are you?"

"I don't know. It kind of depends on how you look at it. Listen, we need a car or a—"

He cut in, "Who's *we?*"

"Claire and I," I told him. "Listen, this call is through the hotel switchboard, isn't it?"

"Shall I call you back, kid?"

"It'd be an idea," I said.

The call came in five minutes. He said, "This is from a booth, Ed. Go ahead."

I said, "Claire and I were getting along, but we had company. A guy named Dutch. Dutch—uh—drank a bit too much and sort of passed out on us. We want to take him home without taking him through the front lobby. It'd be best if he wasn't found here. Now if somebody had a car and parked it in the alley back of here, by the service entrance, and then gave us a hand getting him down the service elevator—"

"Okay, kid. Would a taxi do?"

I said, "The driver might be worried about Dutch. He's pretty—uh—stiff, if you know what I mean."

Uncle Am said, "I guess I know what you mean. Okay, kid, hold the fort. The marines are coming."

I felt a hell of a lot better when I put down the phone and went back to the sofa beside Claire.

She gave me a funny kind of look. She said, "Ed, you called the guy *Uncle* Am. Is he really your uncle?"

I nodded.

She said, "That wild, screwy yarn you pulled about Harry killing your—your father last week and you and your uncle hunting him for that, only your uncle was asleep—wasn't that in with the seven-foot snow on Michigan Boulevard and the dog teams giving out and—"

I said, "It wasn't. It was the straight story. I told that first because I knew you wouldn't believe it, the way I put it. I didn't know where you stood then."

She put her hand in mine again. She said, "You should have told me."

"I did, didn't I? Listen, Claire, think hard. Did you ever hear Harry—or Dutch or Benny—mention the name Hunter?"

"No, Ed. Not that I remember, anyway."

"How long have you known them?"

"Two years. I told you that."

I wanted to believe her. I wanted like hell to believe everything she'd told me. But I had to be sure.

I asked, "Did you ever hear the name Kaufman? George Kaufman?"

She didn't even hesitate. "Yes, about—I guess two or three weeks ago. Harry told me a man named Kaufman might call up this number and give me a message. He said the message could be an address, and I was to copy it down and give it to him. Or that it might be that someone Harry was interested in meeting was at the tavern Kaufman owned. And that if it was that the guy was there, I was to get in touch with Harry quick, if I knew where he was."

"Did Kaufman call?"

"No. Not any time I was here, anyway."

"Could anyone else have taken the message?"

"Harry might have—if it was over a week ago. There would have been times he was here and I was out. Nobody else could have. Ed, this man Harry wanted to meet if he came in Kaufman's—would it have been your father?"

I nodded. It checked; it fitted Kaufman's story like a glove, and proved that both he and Claire were telling the truth about it.

I asked her, "Know anything about Harry's brother, Steve?"

"Only that he's in jail. I think in Indiana. But that was before I met Harry. Ed, I *do* want a drink now. How about you? Can I mix you a Martini? Or would you rather have something else?"

I said, "A Martini would be swell."

When she stood up, she caught sight of herself in the mirror over the mantel. She gasped a little. She said, "I'll—I'll be back in a minute, Ed."

She went through the door behind which I'd hidden not so long ago, and I heard another door open and close and water running. She was feeling better, I knew. When a girl starts worrying about how she looks, she's feeling better.

She came back looking like a million bucks in crisp new currency.

She had a glass of ice cubes and a bottle of vermouth in her hands when the doorbell rang.

I said, "It's Uncle Am. I'll get it."

But I had my hand on the revolver in my coat pocket when I opened the door, on the chain.

It was Uncle Am. He was wearing a taxi-driver's cap, grinning.

He said, "You phone for a cab?"

I unhooked the chain. "Yeah," I said. "Come on in. We got a little packing to do yet."

I closed the door behind him and locked it. He said, "Yeah, you've been doing all right. Wipe that lipstick off your mush and you'll look better, though. Where is it?"

We went into the living room. His eyebrows went up a little when he saw Claire. I saw his lips make the slight involuntary motion toward a whistle that men's lips often make when they look at something like Claire.

Then he turned his head a little and saw Dutch. He winced a little.

He said, "Kid, you should have told me to bring a derrick." He walked over and stood looking down. He said, "No blood, no marks. That's something, anyway. What'd you do, scare him to death?"

I said, "It was almost the other way round. Uncle Am, this is Claire."

She put out her hand and he took it. He said, "Even under the circumstances, it's a pleasure."

She said, "Thanks, Am. A Martini?"

She was already getting out a third glass. Uncle Am turned and looked at me and I knew what he was thinking. I said, "I'm all right. I had two thimblefuls of green ink, but that was several weeks ago. And one rye in the bar downstairs, but that was last year."

She finished the cocktails and handed one to each of us. I sipped mine. It tasted good; I liked it.

Uncle Am said, "How much have you told, Ed?"

"Enough," I told him. "Claire knows what the score is. She's on our team."

He said, "I hope you know what you're doing, Ed."

"I hope so, too," I told him.

"Well, you can tell me all about it tomorrow. There's always another day."

I said, "There's the rest of tonight."

He grinned. He said, "I doubt it. Well, let's get going. Think you can manage half of our drunken friend?"

"I can try."

He turned to Claire. "The cab is in the alley, outside the service door. But it's locked; I came in the front way. You got a key?"

"It opens from the inside. And we can put a piece of cardboard so the catch of the lock will stay back and we can get in again. The elevator will be at the first floor. I think I can run it; I'll go down now and bring it up to the fourth—"

"No," Uncle Am said. "Elevators are noisy—especially ones that aren't supposed to be in use in the middle of the night. We'll get him down those back stairs. You just stay ahead of us so we don't run into anybody. If you see anybody, speak to 'em; we'll hear your voice and stop to wait."

She nodded.

Uncle Am took Dutch's shoulders and I took his feet. He was just too heavy for us to try walking him between us like an ambulating drunk. We'd have to carry him and take our chances.

We got him through the hall and down the stairs. It wasn't a job I'd want to do regularly.

We got all the breaks. The door was like Claire had said it would be. There wasn't anyone around the alley. We got him into the cab, jackknifed on the floor of the back seat, and put over him a blanket Claire had brought down for the purpose.

I sat down and wiped the sweat off my forehead. Uncle Am did, too.

Then he got in behind the wheel and Claire and I got in back.

He said, "Any choice of a final resting place?"

I said, "There's an alley off Franklin—No, skip it; that's the *last* place we'd want to put him."

Claire said, "I know where he used to live, up to a few weeks ago. An apartment building on Division. If we left him in the alley back of there—"

"Smart girl," Uncle Am said. "If there's a tie-in between who he is and where he's found, it'll look less like he's been dropped off there. It'll focus the investigation away from the Milan."

He slid the car into gear.

We came out of the alley on Fairbanks, went north to Erie

and cut over Erie to the boulevard. We stayed in the heavy traffic of the boulevard north to Division Street.

Claire gave him the address and ten minutes later we were rid of Dutch. We didn't waste any time getting out of there.

We hadn't talked any at all. We still didn't talk until we were lost in the boulevard traffic again, heading south. Somewhere a big clock struck two.

Claire was very quiet in a corner of the back seat, with my arm around her.

Uncle Am said, "You still got the gun, kid?"

"Yeah, I got it."

He pulled into the alley, stopped the cab right where it had been before. He said, "Stay in here, you two. Ed, give me the gun and I'll case the joint. If you had company before, there could be someone waiting there. Claire, give me the key."

I wanted to go up with him, but he wouldn't let me.

It was very, very quiet.

Claire said, "Kiss me, Ed."

A little later she said, "I'm taking an early train tomorrow, Ed. I'd—I'd be afraid there, alone. Will you stay, and take me to the train?"

I said, "Chicago is big. Can't you go somewhere else in Chicago, for a while, anyway? Until this is all over?"

"No, Ed. And you've got to promise that you'll never come to Indianapolis looking for me. I won't give you my address. Tomorrow morning's got to be good-bye. For good."

I wanted to argue, but down inside I knew she was right. I don't know how I knew it, but I did.

Uncle Am was opening the door of the taxi. He said, "Break it up, you two. Here's the gun and the key, Ed. Listen, you don't know what that gun's been used for. Keep it tonight, but get rid of it before you come back to the Wacker. And without your prints on it."

I said, "I'm not that dumb, Uncle Am."

"Sometimes I wonder, kid. But you'll grow out of it. When'll I see you again? Around noon?"

"I guess so."

Claire said, "Won't you come up for a drink, Am?"

We were getting out of the cab. Uncle Am opened the front door, and slid into the driver's seat. He said, "I guess not, kids. This taxi and cap are costing me twenty-five bucks an hour and I've had 'em two hours now. That's a little rich for my blood."

Claire said, "Good-bye, Am."

He stepped on the starter of the taxi and then leaned out of the window. He said, "God bless you, my children. Don't do anything I wouldn't do."

He drove off.

We stood there a little while, hand in hand, in the warm summer night, in the darkness of the alley.

Claire said, "It's nice tonight."

I said, "It's going to be nicer."

"Yes, it's going to be nicer, Ed."

She leaned against me a little. I let go her hand and put my arms around her. I kissed her.

After a minute she said, "Shall we go in out of the snow?"

We went in out of the snow.

When I woke up, Claire was dressed already, and was packing a suitcase. I looked at the little electric clock on the bedstand and saw it was only ten o'clock.

She smiled at me and said, "'Morning, Eddie."

I asked, "Is it still snowing out?"

"No, it's all through snowing. I was just going to wake you. There's a train at eleven-fifteen. We'll have to hurry, if we're going to eat any breakfast."

She went to a closet for another suitcase.

I got up, took a quick shower, and dressed. She'd finished packing by then. She said, "We'll have to settle for coffee and doughnuts at the station. There's only an hour now."

"Had I better phone for a cab?"

"There's a stand out in front. At this time of morning, we can get one."

I took the two suitcases and she took the overnight bag and a small package that I saw was stamped for mailing. She saw me glance at it and said, "Birthday present for a friend of mine; I should have mailed it two days ago. Remind me, on the way."

I didn't give a damn about birthday presents. I walked to the door and then turned around, with my back toward it and put down the suitcases.

I held out my arms, but she didn't come. She shook her head slowly. "No, Ed. No good-byes, please. Last night was good-bye for us. And you mustn't ever look for me; you mustn't ever try to follow me."

"Why not, Claire?"

"You'll know why, Ed, when you've had time to think things out. You'll know I'm right. Your uncle will know; maybe he can tell you. I can't."

"But—"

"How old are you, Ed? Really? Twenty?"

"Almost nineteen."

"I'm twenty-nine, Ed. Don't you see that—"

I said, "Yeah, you're practically dying of old age. Your arteries are hardening. Your—"

"Ed, you don't see what I mean. Twenty-nine isn't old, no, but it's not young any more, either, for a woman. And—Ed, I was lying to you last night about the job and the hall bedroom and all that. When a woman's used to good things, and money, she can't go back, Ed. Not unless she's stronger than I am. *I'm* not going back to that, Ed."

"You mean you're going to find yourself another mug like Harry?"

"Not like Harry, no. I have learned that much. A guy with money, but not earned *that* way. I've learned that much in Chicago. Especially last night when Dutch—I'm glad you were here, Eddie."

I said, "Maybe I understand a little. But why can't we—"

"How much do you make, Eddie, as a printer? Do you see?"

"Okay," I said.

I picked up the suitcases and went out. We got a taxi at the stand in front of the hotel, and started for the Dearborn Station.

In the taxi, Claire sat very straight, but I happened to notice that there were tears in her eyes.

I don't know whether it made me feel better or worse. Better, I guess, about last night, and worse about her. I was all mixed up, inside, something like the time Mom had fooled me by being so nice to me, when I came home from going to the carney to get Uncle Am.

I thought, why can't women be consistent? Why can't they be good or bad, and make up their minds which? I thought, I guess most of us are that way, good and bad mixed up, but women are worse and they change back and forth faster. They go to almost absurd lengths of being nice to you, or being nasty.

Claire said, "Five years from now, you'll hardly remember me, Ed."

"I'll remember you," I said.

We crossed Van Buren, under the el, and we were through the Loop, only two blocks from the station.

She said, "Kiss me once more, Ed—if—if you still want to, after I told you the truth."

I still wanted to, and I did. My arms were still around her when the cab stopped. The little package she'd been holding slid to the floor as she moved and I picked it up and handed it to her. I noticed the address, and the name.

I said, "If I hit a million-dollar jackpot, I'll get in touch with you through your girl friend in Miami."

"Don't try, Ed, either for me or for any jackpots. Stick to your job and to being what you are. And don't come in the station with me. Here comes a redcap for my bags."

"But you said—"

"It's almost train time, Ed. *Please* stay in the cab. Mama knows best. Good-bye."

The redcap was picking up the bags and starting away with them.

"Good-bye," I said.

The cabby asked, "Back to the Milan Towers?" and I said, "Yeah," watching Claire walk away from me. She didn't turn around to look back. She stopped at the mailbox outside the door and mailed the package, and didn't turn around at all as she went into the door of the Dearborn Station.

My cab was pulling away from the curb, but I was still looking out. That's how I happened to notice the dark little man get out of the cab that had been right behind mine at the curb, and walk rapidly into the station.

Something bothered me; he looked familiar but I couldn't think where I'd seen him.

We were pulling across the street, turning north into Dear-born Street. I told the driver, "I didn't mean to tell you back to the Milan. I want to go to the Wacker on Clark Street."

He nodded and kept going.

We slowed for a stop light on the next corner, and suddenly I remembered where I'd seen the guy who'd gotten out of the cab behind us. It had been yesterday evening in the bar of the Milan Towers. And he'd been Italian, and I'd thought he looked like a torpedo. I'd wondered if he'd been Benny Rosso—

"Stop," I told the driver. "Let me out here, quick."

He finished crossing the street and pulled to a stop along the line of cars at the curb. He said, "Anything you say, mister. Just make up your mind."

I fumbled a couple of singles out of my wallet and gave them to him. I didn't wait for change. I was out of the cab, running back toward the station. I could get back there quicker on foot than by having the cab go on around the block and wait for lights at every corner.

But it was an awfully long block from Harrison back to Polk. I almost got run down by a car crossing in front of the station, but I kept on running until I was inside the doors.

I stopped running then, and walked fast through the station, looking around. I'd never realized what an enormous place it was. I didn't see Claire and I didn't see the man who might have been following her.

I made two fast circuits of the station and I hadn't seen them, either of them. I hurried up to the information desk. I asked, "Which track is the Indianapolis train on, if it hasn't left?"

"Isn't loading yet. It doesn't pull in until twelve-five."

"The eleven-fifteen," I said. "Has it pulled out already?"

"There's no eleven-fifteen for Indianapolis, sir."

I looked up at the clock; it was fourteen after eleven already. I asked, "What eleven-fifteen trains *are* there?"

"Two of them; the St. Louis Flyer on Track Six, and Number Nineteen on Track One—Ft. Wayne, Columbus, Charleston—"

I turned away.

It was hopeless; two long trains leaving in one minute. I probably wouldn't be able to reach one of them, certainly not both. I didn't have enough money left to buy a fare even to Ft. Wayne.

I looked up and saw the gateman closing the iron gate marked Track Five.

A last desperate chance, I thought. The redcap; if I could find the redcap who took— I looked around and there were a dozen redcaps in sight, in different parts of the station. They didn't all look alike, but I realized I hadn't even looked at the one that had taken her bags. I'd been looking at Claire.

One was walking past me, and I grabbed his arm. I asked, "Did you take two suitcases and an overnight bag for a lady, alone, from a taxi just a little while ago?"

He pushed his cap back and scratched his head. He said, "Well, I mighta. What train?"

"That's what I want to know. It was fifteen minutes ago."

"I—I put a lady on the St. Louie 'bout that long ago, I guess. I don't rightly 'member if she had jest two suitcases and a bag. I—I think there was a violin case, suh."

I said, "Okay, skip it," and gave him a dime. There wouldn't be any use trying to talk to every redcap in the place. By the time I got the right one, he wouldn't remember anyway.

I thought, she might not have been taking a train at all, for all I know. She wouldn't let me come into the station with her. She lied about where she was going, maybe she was lying about the rest of it. Maybe she went out the other door of the station or something.

I sat down on a bench and talked myself into being mad instead of worried. I might have been ten miles off in thinking the guy who got out of the cab had been the same one I'd seen in the Milan. I didn't know our cab had been followed. And if it *was* the guy, it wasn't any more than a wild guess that he'd been following our cab and that he was Rosso. Every Italian in Chicago couldn't be a gunsel named Rosso.

Only I couldn't get mad at Claire.

Sure she'd given me the runaround, but she'd told me she was doing it. She'd told me why.

After last night, I thought, I could never be really mad at Claire. And when I'm married and settled down and have kids and grandkids, I thought, there'd always be just a little bit of love left over for my memory of her.

I got out before I made an ass of myself by starting to bawl or something. I walked over to South Clark and caught a street car north.

CHAPTER 13

I KNOCKED ON THE DOOR of Uncle Am's room and his voice called out, "Come on in," and I did.

He was still in bed.

I asked him, "Did I wake you up, Uncle Am?"

"No, kid, I been awake half an hour or so. I been lying here thinking."

"Claire's gone," I said. "She left town—I think."

"What do you mean, you think?"

I sat down on the edge of the bed. Uncle Am doubled the pillow under his head to raise it up, and he said, "Tell me about it, Ed. Not the personal passages. Skip those, but tell me everything that gal told you about Harry Reynolds, and what happened about Dutch last night, and what happened this morning. Just start at the beginning, from the time you left here yesterday evening."

I told him. When I got through he said, "My God, kid, you've got a memory. But don't you see the holes in it?"

"What holes? You mean Claire changed her story about herself, yeah, but what's that got to do with what we're working on?"

"I don't know, kid. Maybe nothing. I feel old this morning,

this afternoon, whatever it is. I feel like we've been chasing our tails and getting nowhere. Hell, maybe you got more sense than I have. I don't know. I'm worried about Bassett."

"Has he been around?"

"No, that's what worries me. Part of what worries me. Something's wrong, and I don't know what."

"How do you mean, Uncle Am?"

"I don't know how to put it. You're nuts on music; let me put it this way. There's a sour note somewhere in a chord, and you can't find it. You sound each note by itself and it's right, and then you listen to the chord again and it's sour. It's not a major or a minor or a diminished seventh. It's a noise."

"Can you come closer to saying what instrument it is?"

"It's not the trombone, kid. Not you. But listen, kid, it's in my bones; somebody's putting something over on us. I don't know what. I think it's Bassett, but I don't know what."

I said, "Then let's not worry about it. Let's go ahead."

"Go ahead and do what?"

I opened my mouth, and then closed it again. He grinned at me.

He said, "Kid, you're starting to grow up. It's time you learned something."

"What?" I asked.

"When you kiss a woman, wipe off the lipstick."

I wiped it off and grinned back at him. I said, "I'll try to remember, Uncle Am. What are we going to do today?"

"Got any ideas?"

"I guess not."

"Neither have I. Let's take the day off and go slumming down in the Loop. Let's see a movie and then have a good dinner and then go take in a floor show. Yeah, we'll pick one with a good band if there are any. Let's take the day and evening off and get our perspective back."

It was a funny time, that afternoon and evening. We went places, and we enjoyed ourselves, but we didn't. There was a feeling about it like the quietness of the air while the barometer drops before a storm. Even I could feel it. Uncle Am was uneasy like a man waiting for something and not knowing what he's waiting for. For the first time since I'd known him, he was a little crabby. And three times he called the Homicide Department to try to get Bassett, and Bassett wasn't there.

But we didn't talk about it. We talked about the show we saw, and the band, and he told me more about the carney. We didn't talk about Pop at all.

About midnight we called it a day and broke up. I went home. I still felt uneasy. Maybe it was partly the heat. The hot wave was coming back. It was a sultry night and it was going to be hot as the hinges tomorrow.

Mom called out from her room, "That you, Ed?" When I answered, she slipped on a bathrobe and came out. She must have just turned in; she hadn't been asleep yet.

She said, "I'm glad you came home for a change, Ed. I wanted to talk with you."

"What is it, Mom?"

"I was in to the insurance company today. I took them the certificate, and they're putting it through, but the check's got to come from St. Louis and they say it'll be a few days yet. And I'm broke, Ed. Have you got any money?"

"Just a couple of bucks, Mom. I've got twenty-some dollars in that savings account I started."

"Could you lend it to me? Ed, I'll give it back as soon as the insurance check comes through."

"Sure, Mom. Anyway, I'll lend you twenty of it. I'd like to keep the few odd dollars myself. I'll draw it out tomorrow. If you need more than that, I'll bet Bunny could lend you some."

"Bunny was here this evening awhile, but I didn't want to bother him about it. He's worried; his sister in Springfield's going to have an operation early next week. A pretty bad one; he's going to take off work next week and go there, he thinks."

"Oh," I said.

"But if you can give me twenty, Ed, that'll do all right. The man said the check'll be only a few days."

"Okay, Mom. I'll go to the bank first thing tomorrow. 'Night."

I went in and went to bed in my room. It felt funny. I mean, it seemed like I was going back there after having been away for years. It didn't seem like home or anything, though. It was just a familiar room. I wound the clock, but I didn't set it to go off.

Somewhere outside, a clock struck one and I remembered it was Wednesday night. I thought, just about this time a week ago Pop was getting killed.

Somehow it seemed a lot longer time than that. It seemed a year, almost; so much had happened since then. It had only been a week. But I thought too: I've got to get back to work. I can't keep on staying away from work much longer. It's been a week. Next Monday I'll have to go back. Yet going back to work, I thought, would be even stranger than coming back to this room to sleep.

I tried not to think about Claire, and finally I went to sleep.

It was almost eleven when I woke. I dressed and went out to the kitchen. Gardie had gone out somewhere. Mom was making coffee; she looked like she'd just got up.

She said, "There's nothing in the house. If you want to go to the bank now, will you bring some eggs and some bacon back with you, Ed?"

I said "Sure" and went out to the bank and got stuff for breakfast on the way back. Mom cooked it and we'd just about finished eating when the phone rang. I answered it, and it was Uncle Am.

"You up, Ed?"

"Just finished breakfast."

He said, "I finally got Bassett—or he got me. He called up a few minutes ago. He's coming round right away. Something's going to break, Ed. He sounded like the cat that ate the canary."

"I'm coming over," I said. "Leave in a few minutes."

I went back to the table and picked up my coffee to finish it without sitting down. I told Mom I had to meet Uncle Am right away.

She said, "I forgot, Ed. When Bunny was here last night, he wanted to see you, and because he didn't know when or where he could get in touch with you, he left a note. Something in connection with his going down-state next week."

"Where is it?"

"I think I put it on the sideboard, in the living room."

I got it on my way out and read it going down the stairs. Bunny had written: "I guess Madge told you why I'm going to Springfield this week end. You said a guy named Anderz who had sold insurance in Gary had moved to Springfield, and you'd wanted to see him. Want me to look him up while I'm there and interview him for you? If you do, let me know before Sunday, and tell me what questions to ask."

I stuffed the note into my pocket. I'd ask Uncle Am, but he'd said he didn't think the insurance agent would be able to tell us anything. Still, it might be worth a try if Bunny was going anyway.

When I got there, Bassett was just ahead of me. He was sitting on the bed. His eyes looked more tired and washed-out than I'd ever seen them. His clothes looked like they'd been slept in, and yet he looked like he himself needed sleep. He had a flat bottle in his pocket, wrapped in brown paper, twisted above the cork.

My uncle grinned at me. He looked cheerful.

He said, "Hi, kid, shut the door. Frank here is about ready to explode with news, but I told him to hold it till you were here."

It was hot and stuffy in the hotel room. I tossed my hat on the bed, loosened my collar and sat down on the writing desk.

Bassett said, "We got the gang you been looking for. We got Harry Reynolds. We got Benny Rosso. Dutch Reagan is dead. Only—"

"Only," my uncle cut in, "none of 'em killed Wally Hunter."

Bassett had opened his mouth to go on. He closed it again and looked at Uncle Am. Uncle Am grinned at him. He said, "Obvious, my dear Bassett. What else bright and cheerful could you have been going to say with that tone of voice and that look on your ugly mug? You've been letting us pull chestnuts out of the fire for you."

"Nuts," Bassett said. "You didn't get near Harry Reynolds. You never saw him. Did you?"

Uncle Am shook his head. "You're right. We didn't."

Bassett said, "I gave you more credit, Am. I figured you for a smart guy. When you found out Harry'd been interested in your brother and started out after Harry, I gave you rope. I thought you'd lead us to him, maybe."

"But we didn't."

"Nope, you didn't. You disappointed me, Am. You never got to first base. *We* found him. Look, Am, the minute you brought up that gang, I knew they were in the clear. Maybe it was a dirty trick not to tell you, but they were wanted for the bank job in Waupaca, Wisconsin. They'd been identified by Waupaca witnesses. The reward was posted for them. And the Waupaca job was the evening your brother was killed."

Uncle Am said, "Sweet of you, Frank. You got my hundred bucks, and you get the reward, too. Or do you?"

"I don't, damn it. I wasn't the one that got 'em. If it makes you any happier, Am, I been tooken too. Nobody gets the reward on Dutch; he's cold meat. Benny was caught out of the state, and who got Reynolds? The beat coppers!"

"Did you lose much, I hope?"

"Half a G on each of them. They haven't got the Waupaca money yet. Forty grand. There's a ten-percent reward on that. Four G's." He licked his lips. "But hell, it'll turn up in a safe-deposit vault someday on a routine check. There's no lead I can follow to it."

"That's nice," said Uncle Am. "How's about my hundred bucks back? I'm getting low on cash." He opened his wallet and looked into it. "I got only a hundred left out of four hundred I came here with."

"Nuts," said Bassett. "I rode along with you guys; I gave you your money's worth. I told you everything I was going to do."

Uncle Am said, "I'll bet you give it back."

"You'll *bet?*"

"Twenty bucks," Uncle Am said. He took out his wallet again, pulled a twenty out of it. He handed it to me. He said, "The kid'll hold stakes. Twenty says you'll give me that hundred bucks back voluntarily, of your own free will, today."

Bassett looked at him and then at me. His eyes were half closed, hooded. He said, "I should never bet a man at his own game. But—" He took out a twenty and handed it to me.

Uncle Am grinned. He said, "Now how about a drink out of that bottle?"

Bassett took it out of his pocket and opened it. Uncle Am took a long drink and then I took a sip for sociability. Bassett took a long pull and then put the bottle on the floor by the bed.

Uncle Am leaned back against the wall, next to where I sat at the desk. He said, "How did the gang get caught?"

"What's the difference?" Bassett asked. "I told you none of 'em—"

"Sure, but we're curious. Tell us."

Bassett shrugged. "Dutch was found dead early this morning, at dawn, in an alley back of Division. They found Reynolds fast asleep in the building Dutch was back of. Dutch was right under his window."

I leaned forward, and Uncle Am took my arm and pulled me back. He kept hold of my arm.

"How do you figure it?" he asked Bassett.

"Reynolds didn't, that's for sure. Probably Benny. Reynolds would never leave the corpse under his own window. But the whole gang was double-crossing each other. Reynolds' woman—we find she lived at the Milan Towers—crossed the whole bunch of them."

"Who was that?" Uncle Am asked.

"A dame who went by the name of Claire Redmond in Chicago. We think her right name was Elsie Coleman. She came from Indianapolis. According to reports, she was quite a looker."

Uncle Am squeezed my arm tight. His grip said, "Steady, kid." Out loud he asked very casually, "Was?"

"She's dead, too," Bassett said. "Benny killed her last night, and got caught on the spot. It was on a train, in Georgia. We got a long-distance call from there this morning. Benny sang plenty when they caught him cold with a shiv in the dame."

"And the burden of his song?"

Bassett said, "He followed her from Chicago. He and Dutch each figured she had the mazuma and that she and Harry were figuring to cross them. Meanwhile, they must've crossed each other. Benny must have killed Dutch, because he left Dutch's body where it would lead to Harry Reynolds getting caught. Only he doesn't admit that, or hasn't yet."

"You got side-tracked, Frank," Uncle Am said. "Why'd he knife this Elsie-Claire Coleman-Redmond?"

"He thought she was lamming with the dough. Maybe he was right; I don't know. Anyway, he was following her. She had a compartment on the train. Sometime during the night he got in and was searching for the hay. She waked up and yelled and he knifed her. But there happened to be a couple marshals in the car. They nailed him before he could get out of the compartment. But the dough wasn't there."

Uncle Am said, "Hand me the bottle, Frank. I'll have another sip of that mountain dew."

Bassett picked it up and handed it over. He said, "Mountain dew, hell. That's good Scotch."

Uncle Am drank and handed it back. He said, "So what now, Frank. What you going to do now?"

Bassett shrugged. "I don't know. Keep the case on the records. Go to work on something else. Ever occur to you, Am, that maybe this was just a straight holdup-slugging after all, and that we'll never get the guy who did it?"

Uncle Am said, "No, Frank, that never occurred to me."

Bassett took another pull at the bottle. It was half empty already. He said, "Then you're nuts, Am. Listen, if it was anything else, then Madge did it. Incidentally, the insurance company's holding that check till I give them the green light. But I guess the only reason I stalled is I haven't seen this Wilson guy yet. Maybe I'll see him now and get it over with."

He got up, went over to the washbasin. He said, "I'm dirty as a pig. I better clean up a little before I go out again."

He turned on the water. I said to Uncle Am, "Bunny left a note. He's going to Springfield Sunday. He says—here—" I'd found the note by then and handed it to him. He read it and handed it back.

I said, "Shall we have him see the guy?"

Uncle Am shook his head slowly.

He looked at Bassett and took in a long breath and let it out slowly. Bassett was wiping his hands on the towel. He put his glasses in a case in his pocket and rubbed his eyes.

He said, "Well—"

"About that hundred bucks," Uncle Am said. "How would you like to know where to put your hands on that forty grand from Waupaca? Would you pay a hundred bucks to know, even if you had to go out of town to get it?"

"I'll pay a hundred to get four grand, sure. But you're kidding me. How the hell would you know?"

"Pay the hundred bucks," Uncle Am said.

"You're crazy. How could you know?"

"I don't know," Uncle Am said. "But I know a guy who does. And I'll guarantee it."

Bassett stared at him awhile, then his wallet came slowly out of his pocket. He took out five twenties and gave them to Uncle Am. He said, "If this is a runaround, Am—"

Uncle Am said, "Tell him, kid."

Bassett's eyes switched to me. I said, "The money was mailed in Chicago a few minutes after eleven o'clock yesterday. Claire sent it on ahead of her. It was addressed to Elsie Cole, General Delivery, Miami."

Bassett's lips moved, but he didn't say anything I could hear.

I said, "I guess you win your bet, Uncle Am." I handed him the two twenties I had, and he put them in his wallet with the ones Bassett had given him.

Uncle Am said, "Don't take it so hard, Frank. We'll do you one more favor. We'll go over to Bunny Wilson's with you. I've never met the guy."

Bassett came out of it slowly.

CHAPTER 14

IT WAS HOT AS THE Sahara desert and getting hotter every minute as we walked over Grand Avenue. I took off my coat and carried it, and then I took off my hat and carried that, too. I looked at Uncle Am alongside of me and he didn't even look warm. He was wearing a suit coat, a vest, and a hat. There must be a trick to looking as cool as that, I thought.

We crossed the bridge and there wasn't even a breath of breeze off the water.

At Halsted, we went south a block and a half and turned in at the door of Bunny's rooming house. We climbed the stairs and knocked on the door of his room.

Inside I could hear the bed creak. He shuffled to the door in slippers and opened it a crack, then wider when he recognized me.

"Hi," he said. "I was just going to get up. Come in." We all went in.

Bassett leaned against the inside of the door. Uncle Am and I went over and sat down on the bed. The room was like an oven and I loosened my tic and unbuttoned the top button of my shirt. I hoped we wouldn't be here long.

Uncle Am was staring at Bunny with a funny look on his face. He looked puzzled, almost bewildered.

I said, "Bunny, this is my Uncle Am. And this is Mr. Bassett, the police detective working on Pop's case."

I looked at Bunny and couldn't see anything to be puzzled about. He had on a faded dressing gown over whatever he'd been sleeping in, if anything. He needed a shave and his hair was mussed, and he'd obviously had a few drinks the night before. But not enough for a heavy hangover.

Bunny said, "Glad to know you, Bassett. And you, Am; Ed's talked about you a lot."

I said, "My uncle's a little screwy, but he's a good guy."

Bunny got up and walked over to the dresser and I saw there was a bottle there and some glasses. He said, "Will you gentlemen have a—"

Bassett interrupted. He said, "Later, Wilson. Sit down a minute first. I want to check up on that alibi you gave Madge Hunter. I let it go because of another angle. But I want to know now if you can prove what time it was you—"

Uncle Am said, "Shut up, Bassett."

Bassett turned to look at him. His eyes got hot with sudden anger. He said, "Goddam you, Hunter, you stay out of my way or I'll—"

He was taking a step toward the bed, but he stopped when he saw that my uncle wasn't paying any attention to him, none at all. He was still staring at Bunny, with that funny look on his face.

Uncle Am said, "I don't get it, Bunny. You're not what I thought you'd be. You don't look like a killer. But you killed Wally. Didn't you?"

There was a silence you could have cut in chunks.

A long silence.

It stretched out and lasted until it became an answer in itself.

My uncle asked quietly, "You've got the policy here?"

Bunny nodded. He said, "Yeah. In the top drawer there."

Bassett seemed to wake up. He went over to the dresser and pulled open the drawer. He reached under some shirts and groped around. His hand came out with a thick envelope of the type they keep insurance policies in.

He stared at it. He said, "Maybe I'm dumb. How could *he* collect on this? Madge is the beneficiary, ain't she?"

Uncle Ambrose said, "He was planning to marry Madge. He knew she liked him and that she'd be looking for another husband pretty soon. Her type always marries again—she wouldn't have wanted to go back to being a waitress when a guy with a good job like Bunny's wants to support her. And she isn't so young any more and—well, I don't have to draw a diagram, do I?"

Bassett said, "You mean he didn't know about that premium receipt and thought Madge wouldn't know about the policy until after he'd married her? But how'd he account for having hidden the policy?"

Uncle Am said, "He wouldn't have to. After they're married he could pretend to find it somewhere among some stuff of Wally's. And Madge would let him use it for starting his own printing shop; he could talk her into that, because that way it would give them an income for life."

Bunny nodded. "She was always at Wally to get ambitious that way," he said. "But Wally didn't want to."

Uncle Am took off his hat and wiped sweat from his forehead. He didn't look so cool any more. He said, "Bunny, I still don't get it. Unless—Bunny, whose idea was this? Yours—or Wally's?"

Bunny said, "His. Honest. He *wanted* me to kill him, or I'd never even have thought of it. He kept dogging me. I don't mean he ever came right out and said 'Kill me, pal,' but after I took to going around with him and he found out I needed money for my shop, and that I liked Madge and she liked me, he kept *at* me."

Bassett asked, "How do you mean, kept at you?"

"Well, he told me where he kept the policy—in his locker at work, and said nobody else knew about it. He'd say, 'Madge likes you, Bunny. If anything ever happens to me—' Hell, he worked out the whole thing. He told me that *if* something happened to him, it'd be better for Madge if she didn't know about the policy right away, that if she got the money direct she'd head for California or somewhere and blow it in, and he wished he could fix it so she wouldn't know she had the money coming until she was safely married to some guy who could invest it for her."

Bassett said, "But man, that wasn't suggesting you *kill* him. He just said if he died."

Bunny shook his head. "That was what he said, but not what he meant. He told me he wished he had the nerve to kill himself, but that he didn't. That anybody'd be doing him a favor—"

Bassett asked, "What happened that night?"

"Just like I told Ed, up to half past twelve. I took Madge home then, instead of half past one. Afterwards, I figured she wouldn't have known what time it was and if I said one-thirty I'd be protecting both of us.

"I'd given up looking for Wally by then. I knew where there was an all-night poker game on Chicago Avenue over near the river. I was walking up Orleans Street and was almost to Chicago when I met Wally coming the other way. Heading home with four bottles of beer. He was pretty tight.

"He insisted I walk home with him. He gave me one of the bottles to carry. One. He picked the darkest alley to cut through. The street light was out at the other end of it. He quit talking when we started through it. He walked a little ahead of me, and then he took off his hat and carried it in his hand—and, well, he *wanted* me to do it, and if I did I could have Madge and my own shop like I've always wanted and—well, I did."

Bassett asked, "Then why did you—"

My uncle said to him, "Shut up, copper. You've got all you need. Let the guy alone. I understand the whole thing now."

He walked over to the dresser and poured some drinks out of the bottle. He looked at me, but I shook my head. He stopped at three drinks and give the stiffest one to Bunny.

Bunny stood up to drink it. He gulped it down and started for the bathroom door. He was almost there when Bassett seemed to realize what was happening. He yelled, "Hey, don't—" and started across the room to grab the knob of the closing door before it could lock on the inside.

My uncle stumbled into Bassett, and the bathroom door's bolt slid home with a click.

Bassett said, "Goddam it, he's gonna—"

"Sure, Frank," my uncle said. "You got any better ideas? Come on, Ed, let's get out of here."

I wanted out quick, too.

I almost had to run to keep up with him after we were downstairs and out on the sidewalk.

We walked fast, under the blazing afternoon sun. We walked for blocks before he seemed to realize I was there with him.

He slowed down. He looked at me and grinned.

He said, "Weren't we a couple of marks, kid? Going hunting for wolves and catching a rabbit?"

"I wish now we'd never gone hunting."

He said, "So do I. My fault, kid. When I saw that note an hour ago I knew Bunny did it, but I couldn't guess why. I'd never met him, and— Hell, why should I excuse myself? I should have gone to see him alone. But no, I had to grandstand and go along with Bassett."

I asked, "How did the note—? Oh-oh. I see it now, now that I know there's something to see. He spelled the name right; that's what you mean, isn't it?"

Uncle Am nodded. "Anderz. He'd heard it over the phone from you, and you didn't spell it for him. He'd have written it 'Anders' if he hadn't read it on the insurance policy he said he didn't know existed."

I said, "I read the note and didn't see it."

My uncle didn't seem to hear me. He said, "I knew it wasn't suicide. I told you about that psychological quirk of Wally's—he *couldn't* have committed suicide. But I never dreamed he'd gone downhill to where he'd pull a stunt like that. I guess—well, if that's what life did to him, Ed, it's just as well. To play a trick like that on Bunny—"

"He thought he was doing Bunny a favor."

"Let's hope so. He should have known better."

I asked, "How long do you think he'd been planning this?"

"He took out that policy five years ago in Gary. He took that bribe from Reynolds to vote for his brother's acquittal, and then he voted for conviction. He must have figured the Reynolds gang would kill him for that.

"But either something happened to change his mind, that time, or he lost his nerve. He scrammed out of Gary and covered his trail. He couldn't have known Reynolds was here in Chicago, or he wouldn't have bothered with Bunny. He could have gone to Reynolds and had the job done cheaper."

"You mean for five years he's wanted to—"

"He must have kept it in mind, Ed. He kept up the policy, once he had it. Maybe he decided to ride it out until you were through school, started in a good job. Maybe he started working on Bunny about the time you started to work at the Elwood. My God."

We were waiting for lights to change, and I saw we were waiting to cross Michigan Boulevard. We'd walked plenty far, farther than I'd realized.

The lights said, "Walk," and we went across.

My uncle said, "Want a beer, kid?"

I said, "I'll take a Martini. Just one."

"Then I'll give you one in style, Ed. Come on, I'll show you something."

"What?"

"The world without a little red fence around it."

We walked north two blocks on the east side of Michigan Boulevard to the Allerton Hotel. We went in, and there was a special elevator. We rode up a long time, I don't know how many floors, but the Allerton is a tall building.

The top floor was a very swanky cocktail bar. The windows were open and it was cool there. Up as high as that, the breeze was a cool breeze and not something out of a blast furnace.

We took a table by a window on the south side, looking out toward the Loop. It was beautiful in the bright sunshine. The tall, narrow buildings were like fingers reaching toward the sky. It was like something out of a science-fiction story. You couldn't quite believe it, even looking at it.

"Ain't it something, kid?"

"Beautiful as hell," I said. "But it's a clipjoint."

He grinned. The little laughing wrinkles were back in the corners of his eyes.

He said, "It's a fabulous clipjoint, kid. The craziest things can happen in it, and not all of them are bad."

I nodded. I said, "Like Claire."

"Like your bluffing down Kaufman's loogans. Like the swat between the eyes you gave Bassett telling him where the Waupaca money is. He'll spend the rest of his life wondering how you knew."

He chuckled. "Kid, a few days ago you were a bit startled because at your age Wally had fought a duel and had an affair with an editor's wife. You ain't doing so bad yourself, kid. I'm a bit older than you and I've never yet killed a bank robber with a twelve-ounce poker, nor slept with a gun-moll."

"But it's over now," I said. "I've got to go back to work. You going back to the carney?"

"Yeah. And you're going to be a printer?"

"I guess so," I said. "Why not?"

"No reason at all. It's a good trade. Better than being a carney. There's no security in that. You make money sometimes, but you spend it. You live in tents like goddam Bedouins. You never have a home. The food is lousy and when it rains you go nuts. It's a hell of a life."

I felt disappointed. I wasn't going with him, of course, but I'd wanted him to want me to. It was silly, but that's the way it was.

He said, "Yeah, it's a hell of a life, kid. But if you're crazy enough to want to try it, I'd sure like to show you the ropes. You could get along; you've got what it takes."

"Thanks," I said, "But—well—"

"Okay," he said. "I wouldn't talk you into it. I'm going to send a wire to Hoagy and then go back to the Wacker to pack up."

"So long," I said.

We shook hands. He went off and I sat down at the table again and looked out.

The waitress came back and wanted to know if I wanted anything else and I told her I didn't.

I sat there until the shadows of the monstrous buildings got long and the light blue of the lake got darker. The cool breeze came in the open window.

Then I got up, and I was scared as hell that he'd gone without me. I found a phone booth and called the Wacker. I got his room and he was still there.

"It's Ed," I said. "I'm going along."

"I was waiting for you. You took a little longer than I thought."

"I'll rush home and pack a suitcase," I said. "Then shall I meet you at the depot?"

"Kid, we're going back by rattler. I'm broke. Just got a few bucks left for eats on the way."

"Broke?" I asked. "You can't be broke. You had two hundred dollars only a few hours ago."

He laughed. "It's an art, Ed. I told you a carney's money

didn't last long. Listen, I'll meet you at Clark and Grand in an hour. We'll catch a streetcar out to where we can grab a freight."

I hurried home and packed. I was both glad and sorry that Mom and Gardie were out. I left a note for them.

Uncle Am was already at the corner when I got there. He had his suitcase and a trombone case, a new one.

He chuckled when he saw how I looked at it. He said, "A going-away present, kid. With a carney, you can learn to play it. With a carney, the more noise you make, the better. And some day you'll play yourself out of the carney. Harry James' first job was with a circus band."

He wouldn't let me open the case there. We got our streetcar and rode away out. Then we walked to a freight yard and cut across tracks.

He said, "We're bums now, kid. Ever eat a mulligan? We'll make one tomorrow. Tomorrow night we'll be with the carney."

A train was making up. We found an empty boxcar and got in. It was dusk now, and dim inside the car, but I opened the trombone case.

I let out a low whistle and something seemed to come up in my throat and stick there. I knew what had happened to just about all of Uncle Am's two hundred dollars.

It was a professional trombone, about the best one you can get. It was gold-plated and burnished so bright you could have used it for a mirror, and it was a featherweight model. It was the kind of a tram that Teagarden or Dorsey would use.

It was out of this world.

I took it out of the case reverently and put it together. The feel and balance of it were wonderful.

From the trombone playing I'd done in the Gary school, I still remembered the positions for the C-scale. One-seven-four-three—

I put it to my lips and blew till I found the first note. It was fuzzy and sloppy, but that was me, not the trombone. Carefully I worked my way up the scale.

The engine highballed and the jerks of the couplings came along the train toward us and past us, like a series of firecrackers in a bunch. The car started moving slowly. I felt my way back down the scale again, getting more confident with each note. It wasn't going to take me long to be playing it.

Then somebody yelled "Hey!" and I looked and saw my serenade had brought us trouble. A brakeman was trotting alongside the car. He yelled, "Get the hell outa there," and put his hands on the floor of the car to vault inside.

My uncle said, "Give me the horn, kid," and took it out of my hands. He went near the door and put the horn to his lips and blew a godawful Bronx cheer of a note—a down-sliding, horrible-sounding note—as he pushed the slide out toward the brakie's face.

The brakie cussed and let go. He ran alongside a few more steps and then the train was going too fast and he lost ground and dropped behind us.

My uncle handed me back the trombone. We were both laughing.

I managed to stop, and I put the mouthpiece to my lips again. I blew and I got a clear note—a clear, beautiful-as-hell, ringing, resonant tone that was just dumb luck for me to have hit without years of practice.

And then the tone split and it was worse than the horribly bad note Uncle Am had just played for the brakeman.

Uncle Am started laughing, and I tried to blow again but I couldn't because I was laughing too.

For a minute or so we got to laughing at each other, and got worse, and couldn't stop. That's the way the rattler took us out of Chicago, both of us laughing like a couple of idiots.

THE END

DISCUSSION QUESTIONS

- How did Uncle Am's carny background help solve the case?

- Did you think that Ed and Am made a good team? What qualities did both bring to the investigation?

- What kind of person was Wallace Hunter? Did you feel like you got a sense of his character through the details discovered during the investigation into his death?

- What role did the Chicago setting play in the narrative?

- Did any aspects of the plot date the story? If so, which ones?

- Would the story be different if it were set in the present day? If so, how?

- If you were one of the main characters, would you have acted differently at any point in the story?

- Did you identify with any of the characters? If so, who?

- Did this novel remind you of anything else you've read? If so, what?

Dolores Hitchens, *The Cat Saw Murder*
Introduced by Joyce Carol Oates

Dorothy B. Hughes, *Dread Journey*
Introduced by Sarah Weinman
Dorothy B. Hughes, *Ride the Pink Horse*
Introduced by Sara Paretsky
Dorothy B. Hughes, *The So Blue Marble*

W. Bolingbroke Johnson, *The Widening Stain*
Introduced by Nicholas A. Basbanes

Baynard Kendrick, *The Odor of Violets*

Frances and Richard Lockridge, *Death on the Aisle*

John P. Marquand, *Your Turn, Mr. Moto*
Introduced by Lawrence Block

Stuart Palmer, *The Puzzle of the Happy Hooligan*

Otto Penzler, ed., *Golden Age Detective Stories*

Ellery Queen, *The American Gun Mystery*
Ellery Queen, *The Chinese Orange Mystery*
Ellery Queen, *The Dutch Shoe Mystery*
Ellery Queen, *The Egyptian Cross Mystery*
Ellery Queen, *The Siamese Twin Mystery*

Patrick Quentin, *A Puzzle for Fools*
Clayton Rawson, *Death from a Top Hat*

Craig Rice, *Eight Faces at Three*
Introduced by Lisa Lutz
Craig Rice, *Home Sweet Homicide*

Mary Roberts Rinehart, *The Haunted Lady*
Mary Roberts Rinehart, *Miss Pinkerton*
Introduced by Carolyn Hart
Mary Roberts Rinehart, *The Red Lamp*
Mary Roberts Rinehart, *The Wall*

Joel Townsley Rogers, *The Red Right Hand*
Introduced by Joe R. Lansdale

Vincent Starrett, *The Great Hotel Murder*
Introduced by Lyndsay Faye

Cornell Woolrich, *The Bride Wore Black*
Introduced by Eddie Muller
Cornell Woolrich, *Waltz into Darkness*
Introduced by Wallace Stroby